INNATRAEA

Novella Two: Am'ayim

E.R. ZAUGG

This book is dedicated to my child Siri. I hope that you find the power of weaving dreams with your creativity, as you have taught me.

INNATRAEA
NORDRIA
ARA'ASYM ISLES
KIEVAN
ANDALUS
Dwar Mountains
SOPHENE
THAVA
RINOWHN TRIBELANDS
FARUNDIA
FARUN DA'AL
Skywall
SCEOTAN
Djelem'den
TURSIM
Sea of Grass
River Maud
AEDONIA
Porto de la Luce
BETHSEDA
Talberton's Crossing
The Shepherd King
Haversford
Farmhold
Alielle Falls
IMPERIAL SHINODA
Meryl Mountains
The Tanglewood
ROYAL SEYLA
KINRAI
Bay of Swans
AMENG'KHOR
TEOKAHL
0 200 400 600 800 1000
Miles

RENOWHN TRIBELANDS
Feorrker
Victory River
Haversfjord
River Marind
Karum
Sea of Grass
Cove
Altin Bozkirlar
TURSIM
The Tanglewood

Table of Contents

"Ang tunay na kapangyarihan ay nabubuhay sa puso.

Tru powa live inna di haat.

True power lives in the heart."

- Am'ayim Saying

PROLOGUE:
HOUSE MASUDO

*"Di Masudo uman a laik staam, yu
no siel dat Di Saalt ef yu no waan deth.*

*The Masudo women are like storms,
you don't sail those seas unless you want death."*

- Bezalel "Bez" Masudo

Decades earlier . . .

Bez tried to calm himself, which wasn't easy given the circumstances. He swallowed, mouth dry, as Tiare's hand reached down to pick up one of the perfume jars. He'd first met her last night when he and his younger friend Absai had gone to a local tavern, and like an idiot, he'd flirted with and bedded her before knowing who she was. Now, this was his reward. It would have been a glorious fate if it wasn't such a terrible joke.

Bez had heard the Masudo women were crazy, but he'd never expected one to be at a tavern drinking and dancing. He sighed as he watched her lift the clear glass jar off his cart. He looked up to meet her eyes. Tiare Masudo, sister to Ni'moku's matriarch, regarded him evenly.

Her gaze held him like a vice. He may as well have been chained before her like a slave, which he still might be. He couldn't hope but remember the previous evening, the dancing, the alcohol, and her lithe, muscular body against his.

The House Masudo tattoo on her side seemed to glow in the bright sunlight. He had somehow missed it last night and was now paying for that mistake. To think he'd been happy when the woman had appeared at the docks, watching him. He forced himself to look away from her tattooed body and back into her eyes. She smiled, noting where his eyes had been, before opening the perfume bottle and pouring its contents on the ground. The sensuous smell of lily, and vanilla came to his nose as the blue sapphires hit the sandy gravel by his boots.

Absai sighed audibly next to him and looked at Bez sideways as she finally spoke to them both. "Dat a very interestin perfume." Her eyes shifted between them and their full cart of bottles. She smiled, her voice sounding amused of all things, as she waved to the nearby dock guard.

"Dem deh unda arrest. Tek dem tings an put dem inna a cell, mi ago bi kweschan dem miself."

He and Absai put their hands up as the guards approached them; there was no reason to fight now. Sometimes, fate was an inevitable thing. A short time later, they were both shoved into a small cell at the dock master's station. Absai looked at him as they both got up. He spat to the side, rightfully disgruntled. "Dis a yuh fault. Shi wudn bada wi ef yu neva fuck har laas nait. Eediat."

Bez had to laugh; the situation didn't call for much else because his friend was right. "Yu rait mi fren, mi sari." He looked up as they heard the station's door open again. "If mi hab a chance fi tek di blame mi will. Maybe shi let yuh go, yuh a few years younger dan mi."

Then, two guards came in just before Tiare herself. The guards opened the cell without a word and dragged Bez into an adjoining room. There, they sat him in a chair and strapped him down before leaving. He looked up as Tiare entered the room and shut the door behind her with a clang. He tried to look confident as she strode to him and lifted his chin with her hand to make eye contact. "Dis a waan unexpected pleaja." Her eyes held a smoky heat as she smiled. "Yuh good at fucking, mi did hab a gud taim laas nait, bot nuh tink dat earns yuh leniency."

He tried to smile back. "Mi no tink dat, mi did jus a look fi mek some marks pan di side."

She smiled very sweetly, a good indicator that he was in trouble, before sliding her hand between his legs. "Yuh like avoid mi family's tax an call it side money?"

Her eyes held his again and her hand too. He could feel himself responding to that, even though he was very nervous. She was not just dangerous but fatal, beautiful, and powerful. "Maybe yuh tax tu high?" She tightened her grip, noting his physical response, and arched her eyebrow at him. Bez shivered, almost feeling himself convulse, but was barely able to reply. "Dat is . . . mi mean, a lowa tax woulda bring more trade an mek yuh family more marks." She stared at him and moved her hand just a little. "Den maybe, merchants like miself wouldn't need fi mek side marks."

She smiled wickedly and withdrew her hand. He sighed but became nervous once again as she languorously ran her fingers down his arm to one of the straps holding him down. "Mi like yuh Bez, yuh a criminal bot brite tu." She undid that strap and ever so slowly moved to the other one. "Yuh haffi pay fi yuh likkle crime douh . . ." She let those words hang in the air as she undid the second strap, then pulled his hair before forcing him to his feet. The blow to his gut that came next made him fall to his knees in pain, wheezing for breath. She knelt, pulling his hair back again, to meet his eyes. "Yuh an yuh big fren free fi go, but yuh gems a fi mi, fi di inconvenience."

She smiled wickedly again before dropping his head and swaying out of the room. Bez watched her go, still breathing heavily. He had never met a woman like Tiare in his life. She made him want to be more because then he would be good enough for her. A woman like that was worth all the profit of a man's life.

***

Tiare waded into the surf as the powerful waves beat upon her naked body. She was a strong woman. As with any woman in the Masudo family, power was all that mattered to her. She dove beneath the surface, feeling the cold salt water invade every part of her before coming up for air. The sun was only a few hours from setting. Tiare paused while treading water to appreciate its beautiful rays shining upon the waves. Before now, the sea had been the only thing that could make her feel weak, the only thing whose mighty strength engulfed her own. But now . . . now there was Bez.

Years ago, she had let the man go because he'd shown her a good time and had displayed intelligence. Tiare still wasn't sure what had happened after that day. The man had set to life with the will of a sea storm. Earning his own ship, forming a crew from across the islands, trading throughout Innatraea to become one of the highest profiting captains they had, and always bringing the most thoughtful of gifts back to her. Not wealth or gems, she had those, but fragrances, tastes, and words—the things of beauty only he knew she loved. Tiare smiled, feeling the waves as they pushed her naked body around with their rhythm and the sun's warmth on her shoulders. No man had ever pursued her with the single-mindedness of Bez, like she was his fate, and the man knew it.

Tiare shook herself and focused back on the present. She needed a shell, and not just any shell, her kaluluwa, or "soul shell." The unique shell would show Bez how she felt about him. She dove, pushing herself towards the sea floor with powerful strokes, and opened her eyes to the salty underwater world. There were shells everywhere, most shattered, some with creatures still living inside of them, and some too large for her to bring back. She floated there, stroke after stroke, as air bubbles fled to the surface. She gazed out into the cold, harsh sea. And then she saw it, wedged between a large rock and the coral reef. Its inner contours twisted in a colorful spiral, highlighted by the sharp spines around its edges. A bahaghari shell—something rare and possibly deadly if what lived inside was still there. It was the perfect shell, but removing it would take patience and caution. She swam to the surface again to catch her breath, elation rising in her chest. Tiare took a deep breath and dove again.

On her way to the shell, she grabbed a broken piece of ship debris and carried it with her. When dealing with papaka kamatayan, or "death crabs," caution would save your life. She poked the shell gently and it did not move. Placing the debris on it and shaking it gently also produced no response, which meant it was empty. Tiare went to work trying to gently remove it from the crevice in which it was stuck. Shells were fragile, and this one needed to be perfect.

Her lungs screamed for air as she dug. The shell eventually came free into her waiting fingers and it looked beautiful. She swam for the surface, kicking hard. She was proud of herself and couldn't wait for Bez to see her kaluluwa. The irony of Tiare Masudo feeling such things over a man didn't even occur to her in those moments of pure joy.

CHAPTER ONE:
YAUHAN NG TADHANA
(CREW OF DESTINY)

Absai crossed his arms and spat into the water while surveying the work being done. The Ariela was tipped onto her side at the careening wharf, not an unusual task and definitely necessary; it had been a few voyages since her hull had been properly cleaned. He looked down the wharf at Palani and the other watchmen, who were guarding the sheds that currently housed their cargo.

In truth, this was one of the few times he was happy about Bez's connection to House Masudo. Doing this on a beach with their own sailors was an incredibly difficult and expensive task. Here at the wharf, a shore crew took care of Masudo ships. All they had to do was watch and ensure the supply sheds were guarded. Absai spat into the water again. This was also the source of his annoyance, though, House Masudo. They were all crazy, and now his friend Bez, their captain, was going to marry one of them.

Absai still remembered the good old days when it had just been him and Bez making marks any way they could. True, they hadn't had a ship back then and had to work for other captains as they could, but that was the Am'ayim way of life, and they had been free. Everything had changed when Bez met Tiare Masudo. They'd barely gotten out with their skins when she'd caught them trying to smuggle gems past the dock inspectors. She had let them go because she liked Bez but had kept their gems. This seemed like thievery to Absai, but Bez seemed to think it a fair trade.

After that, things started innocently enough, with Bez making sure all their goods were reported to Tiare so he could flirt with her. Then he'd asked Absai to stop coming along for those meetings, which was ludicrous because you never did business with a Masudo alone. Of course, Absai had decided to go anyway, and he quickly discovered what his addle-brained friend was actually doing. After that, the man went to work with a will unlike anything Absai had ever seen.

Before he knew it, they were running their ship under the House Masudo flag and recruiting their own crew. It had happened like lightning in a sea storm. Before this, Absai hadn't realized how many people knew Bez and who held him in high regard around the island. Crew members seemed to materialize every time they needed them. It started with their ship's cook, Nikau, a master cook, then Manaia and Ahohako, who were both very experienced sailors. Then, with Palani, a champion Kali fighter and one of the best watchmen on the islands, and most recently, among many others, a South Islander woman named Fatiou, who would make a decent quartermaster.

As myths of the Ariela's journeys and success spread, people began to speak words Absai had never expected in relation to him and his friend. Words like Yauhan ng tadhana, an ancient phrase among Am'ayim that meant "crew of destiny." Whispers of Bez being a legendary captain began to surface after a few years of success. Bez's meetings with Tiare Masudo also became commonplace. She began seeking him out or waiting for them at the dock.

Absai didn't know about any of that legendary captain stuff and wasn't a fan of House Masudo, but his friend needed him, and he'd sail into Tubig ng Tadhana, or the "Tides of Doom," for Bez. He looked around the wharf again, at the shore crew cleaning their ship and the watchmen guarding the supply sheds, before sighing and spitting into the water. If he was being honest with himself, Absai often found himself starting to believe the stories about Bez and their legendary crew.

Of course, this was both good and bad.

He looked back towards the Ariela, noting that the shore crew was unwinding the capstans so they could turn her about. The good thing was that their crew didn't have to do this backbreaking work. But Absai was a South Islander, and he missed being free to sail as he chose and do what he wanted to with their profits.

Absai remembered a conversation they'd had just after he'd been caught spying, where he'd told his friend that he didn't think getting in bed with a Masudo was a good idea. Bez had laughed and said some men loved soft women while others preferred stingrays. If only his friend's love for stingrays hadn't affected them all.

When they arrived at the port, Tiare had been waiting for them. She had knelt before Bez and closed her eyes for a few moments as if nervous. And nothing made a Masudo woman nervous. Then she opened her palms and presented the bahaghari shell to him. His friend had taken the deadly shell from her, dipped it into the bay and drunk seawater from it without hesitation, smiling like a madman the whole time. Absai needed to get drunk tonight and maybe find himself a woman, not the marrying kind, though, the ones you paid and never spoke to again. His friend was crazy.

***

Hiraya walked to the edge of Bundok ng Mga Reyna, her family's stone dais on the north end of Ni'Moku and looked out over her island. Most called this "The Stone of Queens" because it was the true seat of Masudo power. Where new Reyna's ascended, where past mothers were buried, and where marriages took place. And it was here that the lucky few men who won a Masudo's heart were accepted into their dynasty and took on the family name. From that moment onward, any other women they married and any children they had all belonged to House Masudo. It was a great honor. Fortunes, wars, and history were made in pursuit of that honor.

From here, she could see over the entire island—her island. From western coasts to eastern bays, from southern reefs to northern mountains. Hiraya touched the stone that represented her mother and closed her eyes. A single tear fell, but only the one this time. It had been many years and Hiraya had been the dynasty's Reyna for just as long. She smiled and tilted her face up to enjoy the warm sun. Today, they were here for a happier purpose. She hoped that her mother's soul would bear witness to this joyous occasion, a rare one in dynasty history.

Before the sun set, Bundok ng Mga Reyna would see the second marriage in one generation. In House Masudo, where women held power, sisters did not survive, but Hiraya's had. Perhaps it was because of the grief they had both felt upon losing their mother when they were so young, or perhaps it was their love for each other. Hiraya opened her eyes and smiled, knowing the truth was probably a little of both. What was important today was that her sister Tiare had chosen a man, and their marriage was imminent.

Hiraya turned around and started pacing the dais, making sure that everything had been appropriately arranged by the servants. Their eyes traced her as she moved. Of course, this was an important occasion, and the servants were nervous. She made a few minor adjustments: a shell just out of place, flowers disarranged, or a gathering of lei that wasn't neat enough. She looked down the slope and saw her dear Isagani coming. He had been chosen as the Aratohu for this event, a role normally reserved for the bride's father. But like their mother, he too was lost to them. Not far behind him would be Tiare and her chosen husband, followed by the rest of their guests. She smiled and nodded. "Unu aal du gud inna yuh preparations, tank yuh all." She could feel the servants relax, swelling with pride and smiling. Today was for joy and happiness.

Then Tiare came into view. She looked stunning in her seashell-adorned silk dress. It had taken months to make, and every moment was worth it as the sun shone down, lighting her sister's smile. The Masudo Korowai—a feathered cloak passed down through generations of their women—rested upon Tiare's shoulders and seemed to ripple in the wind as if alive. Had Hiraya herself looked so beautiful on her wedding day?

Tiare stepped onto the dais as she followed Isagani to her place beside Hiraya. The wind gently played with her sister's hair as if to say this bride was so beautiful that even the elements encouraged her joy. Then, her sister's chosen husband came into view, Bez. Hiraya forced herself to keep smiling and not grimace like she wanted to. He was handsome enough and had proven loyal to House Masudo, but he had been a criminal when he'd first met her sister and Hiraya wasn't fully convinced Bez had changed much over the years. In her mind, the man was still a miscreant who smoked too much Haze Flower and did as he pleased, even if he turned an astonishing profit for them. She sighed quietly and kept her smile in place. He stopped at the dais' edge while everyone took their places. She would say nothing. Years ago, she and Tiare decided to support one another in everything, and even after Hiraya's initial objections, her sister continued to court Bez. Tiare truly loved the man, and he had proven loyal, so Hiraya smiled and said nothing. Today was for joy and happiness.

Chapter Two: Kasarena (Wedding)

"Marenatia te tangata e mau mai ai te rongo ki te moana. Ma te marama me te mahana e manaakitia ai to aroha. Whiria te tangata.

Marry di man weh bring peace tuh yuh ocean. Mek yuh luv's fate be bless by lite an warmth. Weave di people dem tugeda.

Marry the man who brings peace to your ocean. Make your love's fate be blessed by light and warmth. Weave the people together."

- Masudo Family Wedding Blessing

Bez thought he had known how beautiful Tiare was, but he was wrong. When he stepped onto the great stone dais, a place few men were ever allowed, he saw her, and his mouth went dry. He had seen her muscular, tanned body before, but now it was accentuated by her magnificent red silk dress and the many colored seashells that adorned it. As she met his eyes, the wind lifted her hair, sending it into disarray. She reached up to put it back into place nervously. Nothing made Tiare nervous. When she looked back at him again, she smiled, and the sun turned her eyes into deep pools of brown gold. When Bez was first told of the Masudo wedding ceremony, he didn't like the idea of approaching his new wife on his knees, even if she was Tiare Masudo; he was a sea captain. But now he fell onto his knees anyway, struck down by her powerful beauty and strength.

Their eyes held one another and everything else left Bez's mind. There were things he was supposed to do, but he couldn't concentrate on anything but her. He could feel the wind blowing across the dais, rustling his hair and brushing over his bare chest. The sun felt warm on his back. The wind blew Tiare's hair into disarray again and ruffled the colorful feathers of her cloak. She reached up to fix it while glancing away as her sister Hiraya leaned in to whisper something. They laughed quietly together and though Bez couldn't hear the joke, he was sure it was about him. The wind picked up briefly, and some clarity returned in those moments as Bez looked around the dais, remembering where he was.

Some of the Ariela's crew were there. He hadn't liked the idea, especially after learning how this ceremony would go, but it was an even worse idea to insult his new wife-to-be. He was allowed to invite four, so he did: Absai, Nikau, Manaia, and Ahohako were all present. They were trying to act polite and proper, but he could see the amusement behind their eyes. He would never hear the end of this. Then, his eyes fell upon the fifth crew member. She was new to the Ariela, and he hadn't invited her, but it was apparently Masudo tradition for all women crew to attend. Oddly, when he looked at Fatiou, there was a surprising level of respect in her gaze. He only recognized some of the others present, mostly House Masudo, friends of the family, trade partners, or servants. Sighing, he placed his hands on the stone before him. Bez looked at Absai one last time to make sure he was still holding the ornate box he'd given his old friend earlier, and then he closed his eyes for just a moment. It was time to focus.

When Bez opened his eyes and looked up, he saw Tiare. Her curious gaze was on that box, and then she looked back at him and nodded. It was time. His heartbeat was so loud that he was afraid his heart would burst. Finally, Hiraya spoke and her voice seemed to echo across the dais like thunder. "Ka mauria mai e koe te rangimarie o tana moana?" The words took him a moment to decipher as he spent more time away from the islands now than at home. *"Yuh promise fi always bring peace to har ocean?"*

Bez's mind drifted back to when Tiare explained the Masudo wedding ceremony to him. *"Shi ago ask yuh kweschan, dem as yuh approach wi, yuh haffi stay humble an gib yuh own ansa dem. Dis a very important Bez."* Her eyes showed love and faith but also a demand for him to respect their ways. *"Di fos kweschan about peace. Masudo uman a laik sii staam, az yu nuo. A husband haffi always bring peace to har ocean."*

Bez looked up and met Hiraya's eyes, though he stayed on the ground. He wanted to look at Tiare and say he was doing this for her, but he wasn't supposed to, not yet. "Mi a waan sea kyapten. Mi haffi andastan Di Saalt, ship, an crew." He pressed on even though he had been worried about speaking these words in the common tongue. He was a captain and not home often. His words were more eloquent this way. "Dis a how mi andastan di world. Mi wi gib evriting mi hav fi bi di same fi mi waif, az lang az wi a liv."

The wind seemed to still as quiet fell over the dais like a cloud. Bez tried to wait patiently and calmly to meet Hiraya's eyes, but there was too much judgment there. It was as if the weather and even Innatraea herself bent to this woman's will, and now she was weighing his words, deciding the worth of his heart. Finally, she nodded, and Bez breathed out, releasing some of the tension in his body. Before he lowered his gaze and crawled forward again, Bez glanced at Tiare. She smiled at him with love and respect in her eyes.

After what seemed like a few more feet, Hiraya's voice boomed over the dais again, and Bez stopped to listen. "E whakapono ana koe ko ia to mate?" "*Yuh believe seh shi a yuh fate?*" An Am'ayim woman deserved to know that a man really loved her and understood she was the fate of his heart, and this was especially true of the Masudo family.

Bez sat up on his knees again, looking Hiraya in the eyes. He was careful not to look at Tiare again, even though he really wanted to. Eventually, this ceremony would end, and they would only be with each other. But this was required of him first, to show her how much he loved and respected her with all his heart. "Wen mi fos miit Tiare mi neva shuor." He could almost feel Tiare's gaze sharpen upon hearing his words, but he didn't look at her for fear of hesitating. Instead, he forced himself to continue. A captain had to sail rough seas sometimes, and women were no different. It felt like the wind was picking up as Bez started talking again. It may have just been his imagination. "A afta dat, wen she ketch mi a try smuggle gems dat mi get shuor."

He smiled, remembering that day, and imagined Tiare's gaze softening. "Shi did have mi, an even though shi punish mi, shi did kind an mek mi go. Mi naa go eva figet har powa, waan uman laik dat a waan sain a fiet fi eni man." He looked at Tiare and smiled. She did not smile in return, but there was a fierce glow of passion in her eyes. "Bot shi pik mi bifuo dat, iivn duo shi neva nuo it, an mek mi go. Tiare is mi fate."

Bez turned his head towards Tiare's sister, Hiraya. Moments passed. He could feel his heart beating faster, could feel the wind blowing through his hair, and finally, she nodded. Without another word, he lowered himself to his hands and knees and started crawling towards them. When he reached the two women, Bez stopped and waited. He could still feel the wind, hear his own heart beating, and almost sense the crew's future laughter. But he wanted to marry Tiare Masudo with all of his being, so he waited and breathed.

They hadn't told Bez what was going to come next. Only that he was to approach on his hands and knees while answering Hiraya's questions as part of the wedding blessing. Then Tiare spoke, and there was a feeling of love and warmth in her voice. "Tan up." Bez sprang to his feet without a second thought. His future wife, his love, had told him to stand. She raised her hands and there was a coin in each of her open palms. She met his eyes, and there was a mixture of emotions: love, respect, and hope. "Whiria te tangata. *Weave di people dem tugeda.*"

Another test. Their entire relationship up until now had been this way. In truth, he had expected as much. Tiare was a strong and challenging woman and Bez loved that about her. He looked at the two coins carefully, considering. One showed a ship and the other House Masudo's Imperial Hand. Perhaps he was supposed to symbolically give up his old life for his new one? He reached for the House Masudo coin. The coins vanished as Tiare closed her fists. In an instant, the breath was knocked out of him. His knees buckled as both women hit him in the gut and sides. Wheezing, Bez tried to gather his thoughts. *"Whiria te tangata."* *Weave di people dem tugeda.*

Bez sat up and smiled, finally knowing what to do. There was no specific ritual here. It was his moment to show Tiare she was loved that he could weave their lives together, and that he deserved her. Instead of getting up again, Bez motioned for Absai to bring him the box. He could feel Tiare and her sister Hiraya watching him as his old friend cautiously approached and handed him the ornate box. Bez carefully took it into his hands and turned back towards Tiare. Her eyes traced his movements with an intense curiosity. Many men had spent their lives and fortunes pursuing the women of House Masudo, and in truth, this had cost him enough for a second or even third ship. But Bez knew her, deep down into her soul, and so he'd chosen differently. Where most men chose wealth, gems, gold, or power: all things the women of House Masudo had on their own. Bez had chosen beauty. Something that would touch Tiare in her soul. He slowly opened the box.

Tiare's eyes lit up like the sun. He didn't have to speak a word. She knew what it was, how much it must have cost him, and what it meant. A Nordrian Ice Rose, perfectly preserved by Weaver's magic and brought home to her. They were the rarest flowers on all of Innatraea; they only bloomed in the hearts of the most deadly northern winters. This was the only thing in all of Innatraea that Bez could imagine equaled his love.

She came to him, and all pretense was gone. She leaned over and embraced him. Her arms closed around Bez as her lips met his. The wind picked up and blew her feathered cloak around them both. It was the perfect moment. Even more importantly, she was his now. He didn't hear Hiraya step forward, speak the final wedding vows, or feel the marriage lei fall around his neck; there was nothing else in his world now except her.

CHAPTER THREE: THE FLOWER OF NI'MOKU

"Ko te ngakau o te kotiro to tatou kaha.

A daughta haat a fi wi powa.

A daughter's heart is our power."

- Masudo Family Creed

Bez removed his fingers from his lips and opened his eyes before putting his paipa back in his mouth. They were drifting past Babe ng Asin, or the "Woman of Salt," a statue that depicted a woman and child, marking entry into the Ara'ayim Isles, his people's home. You were supposed to calmly pay respect to the statue and think about your life, especially how you treated others, but Bez was completely distracted. This voyage had taken longer than expected, and Tiare was pregnant again when he left. He looked into the sky and carefully touched his lips again, praying for Lux's benevolence. He'd already given Tiare two sons, though she still said words of love and hadn't lost patience with him yet, he also knew that a daughter would mean everything to her. Especially since her sister Hiraya, whose husband was now long dead, hadn't ever produced an heir. Only women could inherit the power of House Masudo. A daughter meant everything now.

The Ariela was moving too slowly. He turned on the crew abruptly and said, "Unu all a move slower dan a Caim blessed huddle a walruses!" He regretted it almost immediately as Absai looked at him with a raised eyebrow. Bez sighed. He was just in a hurry and knew the crew understood.

In fact, he had already heard Manaia joking to Ahohako about how their captain better hope the baby was a girl or his wife would gut him like an ahi. The men laughed and slapped the other's shoulders before they both looked at Bez and got back to work. Absai crossed his arms and nodded. "Dem a joke. Bot yuh shuor Tiare naa go tek yuh balls if yuh fail har again?"

Bez laughed and took another few puffs of his paipa before replying. Haze Flower helped calm his nerves. "Mi no shuor, but mi tink dis time mi inna trouble."

Absai slapped him on the shoulder before walking away to check on things for docking. They were almost there, one more island to sail around and then home would be in sight. Ni'Moku, the Isle of Birds, is one of the largest islands in the chain and is the base of power for House Masudo. He smoked the last dregs of his paipa and tapped it out on the railing before putting it in his pocket. It was almost time. He was always excited about going home and truly loved his wife, but only wise men survived around the Masudo women.

Bez walked to the foredeck and crossed his arms. He tried to look calm as the Ariela sailed around Ni'Mautuba. Ni'Moku came into sight, and he felt his stomach clench. He couldn't wait to see Tiare and their baby, but he was always nervous when coming in from a journey. This one had been profitable, though, and Lux sent that they now had a daughter. He touched his lips again as the Ariela cleared Cape Kamay, bringing his home into sight.

Ni'Moku came into sight and Bez sighed, releasing the tension from his shoulders. He was home and whatever was destined would come. He smiled, closed his eyes and took a deep breath. He opened them and looked over the city and docks. There were throngs of people watching the Ariela approach. He knew that word of any ship coming passed quickly among the islands, using their signaling towers, and his wife was always there to meet him, but this wasn't usual.

As the Ariela came closer to the docks, the people parted, and two women started walking towards where they would dock. Bez immediately recognized his wife Tiare and her sister Hiraya. His wife was carrying a small bundle in her arms. The people started throwing waling-waling blossoms over the two women as they walked to meet the Ariela. Tiare stopped at the dock's edge and raised their new baby into the air, who started crying as the wind surrounded her in red and white waling-waling blossoms. Bez fell forward, catching himself on the ship's railing. He knew what this meant. Not only did they have a daughter now, but she had also been named The Flower of Ni'Moku, heiress to House Masudo.

***

Tiare lifted her baby girl into the air and smiled, ignoring the weakness in her limbs. She could still feel the salt and blood from giving birth to her daughter in the surf and her husband needed to know. Their daughter's name was Rangi, which meant "Of the Sky." It was a powerful name, Lux-blessed and meant for great things. Tiare watched Bez catch himself on the ship's railing as the Ariela neared. He knew what this meant. She wanted to scream, laugh, cry, dance, and bed her husband because now the family had an heiress and she was theirs. As if to answer her thoughts, a sharp wind blew through Kokoru Ista, the central bay of Ni'Moku, better known as the "Bay of Fish," and swirled the waling-waling blossoms around her daughter.

Hiraya leaned closer while gently placing her hand on Tiare for support as she brought her newborn daughter back against her breast. "No tell har how much signs a fate did a go wid har birth." Hiraya looked towards the Ariela as it started docking and smiled. "Shi a waan Masudo uman aredi, knowing seh shi fated ago mek har insufferable."

Tiare hadn't felt this happy for a very long time. "Mi a hope seh she a waan Caim blessed challenge fi all a wi. Mi feel like fi wi people dem ago need dat." She saw her husband heading towards the gangplank. "Somting difrent deh pan di winds lately."

Hiraya nodded, also watching Bez approach. "Yu rait sista, mi a fiil di difrent winda dem tu, mi a wori bout wi piipl dem fyuucha tu." She looked at Rangi and smiled. "Mi a uop fi di siem ting laik yuh." She looked up again as Bez's feet hit the dock and he headed towards them. "Yuh may find out seh ada umen dem interested inna him line, now dat him know as di fada a House Masudo's next Reyna."

Tiare held her daughter closer. "Im a waan smaat man, im nuo im duty." Then Bez was there, wrapping his arms around her and kissing Rangi on her little forehead. Hiraya stepped away to watch the Ariela be unloaded. After a few moments of fervent kissing, Bez stepped back to truly look at their daughter. Tiare held her up for him. It was important that a man bond with his child early. "Har name a Rangi, a name a powa."

Bez took their daughter into his arms, holding her up for just a moment, before laying her against his bare muscled chest and smiling proudly. "Shi priti an strang."

She thought back to the past and how Bez had courted her. As if the man had known, she was his fate. Tiare gently laid a hand on her daughter's head while meeting her husband's eyes. She loved him so much. "Shi strang, an shi naa go onlu nuo har mada an har House Masudo heritij, bot shi a go nuo di kain a man we mek har tu." Bez smiled even more proudly, but Tiare also heard a sharp intake of breath from her sister Hiraya. She'd obviously said the wrong thing. No Masudo glorified the men in their lives, but she didn't care. Bez had pursued her as if the winds of destiny were his guide and their daughter was fated. Perhaps it was time for other things to change.

***

That evening, Hiraya walked out onto Bangin ng Tagak, her balcony better known as "Heron's Rest," named so for the mighty birds that had once nested there long ago. The evening sun was just touching the sea's horizon and lit the entire bay with golden amber light. She stopped at the railing and gently placed her hands there to watch the sun go down. This was her favorite time of day. Today had been an auspicious one and yet she still felt that familiar internal pang of regret.

She had never been able to birth an heiress and her Isagani had died at sea years ago. True, she was allowed to bed other men and could have their children, but they would not be born blessed by marriage and able to inherit her power. Marrying again was also not a choice she could make; it would dishonor what she had given her dear Isagani when choosing his hand. This doom had been a weight upon her shoulders since his death years ago, and it had been a heavy one. She would never admit this to anyone as Masudo women were not weak, but this had caused her many tears of shame over the years. The sun was nearly half down, bathing her in its warm light as if Lux's hand was reaching out to comfort her against those past sorrows. Hiraya unclenched her fists and wiped the tears from her eyes. They had an heiress, and House Masudo would live on. Even though Rangi wasn't her own, she would do everything in her power to protect her sister's baby girl. The child meant everything to them now—their next Reyna.

This brought on a new line of thought as her eyes traveled back over the bay. Her sister had said that Rangi would also know her father, the kind of man that made her as if that was something that truly mattered to Tiare. Why? No Masudo heiress was ever taught their father's world; that was not the way things were. She was especially displeased because, truthfully, she had never much liked Bez. True, he had proven himself a loyal husband and very successful captain, but the man was a miscreant and spent too much of his time smoking Haze Flower for Hiraya's liking.

What strange fate did the winds and tides have in store for them? Hiraya suddenly felt as though this specific peaceful evening might be her last. The sun dipped below the horizon, bathing her world in quiet shadow as Hiraya's fists clenched again.

CHAPTER FOUR:
ATUENO NGAKAU
(FATED HEARTS)

"Ko nga ngakau whakatapua kaha e hanga ana i to ratau aitua.

Strang haats shape dem wun fates.

Strong hearts shape their own fates."

- Am'ayim Saying

Bez watched his little girl, Rangi, charge into the ring, screaming. She was going to be just as beautiful as her mother one day. She had the same large dark brown eyes, black hair, and pointy chin. They even had the same hairstyle—short and braided tightly. Good for fighting. She was five years old now and the most important of his children because she was the Masudo heiress, their next Reyna.

Rangi leaped onto her opponent's back, a boy who was a few years older, and started beating him with her fists and elbows while screaming, "Shi a waan Caim blessed likkle terror!"

Tiare crossed her arms and looked over at him, smiling proudly. She was such a beautiful woman. Her lithe, muscled body always excited him, especially when they were home or aboard a ship and she went shirtless. The sun caught her dark brown eyes, turning them into twin amber flames. "Yeah, shi priti an strang."

The boy finally left the ring, crying, and his daughter ran over to them. "Fada! Yuh si mi? Mi beat him up gud!"

Bez knelt down, smiling, and hugged her. "Mi si dat, yuh did a gud job." Rangi's face lit up with such a big smile he couldn't help but laugh.

Tiare looked down at them, mildly amused. "Rangi, go do yuh stretches an exercises."

"No! Mi waan spen taim wid mi fada wail im de a yaad!"

Tiare arched her eyebrow at their daughter. In response, Rangi crossed her arms and looked back defiantly. "Kom wid mi pikni," Tiare told her as she walked into the ring. "If yuh can touch mi wid yuh fist yuh can spen time wid yuh fada."

Rangi barreled into the ring right behind her mother, screaming. Apparently, fighting also involved their daughter making as much noise as possible. Bez laughed. Some men might find playing audience to women like this demeaning, but he loved it. There was an attractive quality in a strong, intelligent, and brutal woman.

Rangi was circling her mother, testing her defenses carefully. His little girl would jump in, feigning a strike, see her mother move, and jump back out. A strange dance for a child, but she was a Masudo, and they were different. The Masudos were an entire family of women who were natural-born leaders, understood the politics of trade, and were more deadly than a hurricane. Bez loved them. He never regretted marrying into the Masudo family.

Rangi dove in again, first going for a side strike. Her mother moved to block and his little girl spun around her mother's arm, then kicked her in the side. Tiare stopped. The blow wasn't bad since Rangi was still small, but her daughter had struck her for the first time. There were tears of pride in her eyes. "Amazing Rangi, yuh ago be a champion. Mi was ten before mi coulda strike mi own mada. Go aan, enjai di taim wid yu fada wail im de a yaad."

Rangi ran to him and leaped into his arms. "Yuh si dat deh fada? Mi did do it!"

"Aye, mi si dat, mi very proud a yuh. Weh yuh waan do?"

Rangi's face lit up. "Mi waan see yuh ship! Di Ariela!"

***

Bayani looked out into the harbor longingly. All he wanted was to be on a ship, sailing with his people. He was stuck here, however, because he'd been born a shore child. Somehow, it was his fault that his mother was a poor prostitute who'd met an Am'ayim sailor, given birth to him, and then died. Now he was stuck here, scraping by as a street orphan and pickpocket, in Kinrai. Someday, he'd get to be on a ship. It was his dream!

Bayani stood up. He needed to get going. If he were late with the day's take, then Armis would be upset with him. Plus, he wanted to head into the Am'ayim quarter and ask old Mataalii about training in Kali again. The old man owned the only place in Kinrai that taught the fighting style. Kali was a traditional Am'ayim style, and he wanted to learn it badly. It would help him become a real Am'ayim. He couldn't stay here, living on the streets and giving everything he had to others.

He walked down the nearest alley, kicking garbage out of his way while daydreaming about a better life. It was not the best habit for a street orphan in this city, but he was prone to distraction. Maybe that's why the old man wouldn't teach him? Suddenly, there was someone in his way. Bayani looked up into the strange man's eyes. He had short brown hair and light brown eyes and was dressed like a farmer.

Bayani's instinct was to run. People weren't kind to street orphans. The man held up a gold mark and then squatted down to talk with him. "Hello there. Bayani right? I have something for you." He held out a pouch full of marks. "Take them, they're yours. You can pay the old man and your daily take for quite some time."

Bayani was suspicious. "What do you want? Why are you helping me? Are you some creep? How do you know my name!?"

The man laughed and smiled. "Nothing like that. I see potential in you; you're a smart kid and talented. I know your name because I'm an old family friend. I'm sorry it took me so long to find you. Kinrai doesn't keep very good track of its orphans."

Bayani carefully reached out and took the pouch while watching the man warily. He was surprised. The man actually just let him take the pouch. Bayani had never laid hands on so many marks in his life! The man smiled. "I have to go now. Be careful with that and take care of yourself. We'll meet again someday."

Bayani watched the man leave. He wasn't sure what to do or say. The man walked around a corner, and when Bayani was finally able to move, he chased after him to say thank you. The man was gone when he rounded the corner. He had vanished like a ghost.

***

Thirteen years later...

Rangi looked at her mother defiantly. "Mi a waan big piipl nou, mi kyan du eniting mi waan! Unu kyaahn stap mi!"

Tiare glared back. "Di uman dem a House Masudo a nuh common sailors!"

Rangi crossed her arms and met her mother's eyes. "Unu no andastan!"

Bez leaned against a nearby wall, lamenting his general existence. No man ever told a Masudo woman what to do. Being here, witnessing his wife and daughter argue, felt like testing the waters against Caim himself. He dared not even light his paipa because it might draw their attention. So he stood there, trying to look calm, when really he was as nervous as a brand new ship's cat. Hopefully, if he were quiet enough, this ship's cat wouldn't be skinned alive.

Tiare crossed her arms, her voice sounding like a knife dragged across the stone. "Den explain it to mi, daughta."

Rangi nodded and pointed directly at Bez. Tiare's baleful stare followed, so much for being quiet and unseen. "Di Am'ayim dem a sailors an mi fada a di kyapten a waan ship. Mi a Am'ayim an mi ago go wid im!"

Tiare uncrossed her arms and nodded, stepping into the ring. The women of House Masudo were a unique breed. Nothing her daughter said was going to convince her, but at least this statement had granted Rangi the right to challenge, which was her goal all along. Rangi stepped into the ring with her mother and took a stance. Her eyes had a look of determination. Rangi never failed at anything when she had that look.

They moved, collapsing into each other like two whirlwinds of fists, elbows, and legs. He could barely keep track of what was happening. It looked like pure chaos, accompanied by the sound of muscle and bone striking flesh. Bez leaned forward, enthralled. Sayaw ng Kamatayan, or the "Dance of Death," was as dangerous as it was beautiful, and these two women were its masters. A pressure filled the air. Bez waited for the stillness of a winning strike, the pressure building more with each blow until finally, it stopped. The women froze. Rangi's fist was flat against her mother's torso, the winning strike.

The women locked eyes, and Tiare nodded. The decision was made. Rangi left the ring and looked at Bez. She was bloodied and bruised, but her face had the purest look of love and pride he'd ever seen. He fumbled the earring out of his pocket as she came close and held it up. It's what she wanted, not a hug or him saying how proud he was. She wanted the earring of a sailor on his ship, the Ariela.

***

Bayani watched the crew as they were unloading. It was hard work, but they were Am'ayim; it was their way. He took a deep breath. This was the ship he'd chosen. He had spent over ten years preparing for this moment and it was time to throw the knife. He wanted to be a sailor . . . needed to be a sailor. He was Am'ayim, too. He'd been born a shore child, away from the water, but he'd still learned Kali and that meant he was strong. He looked at the ship. She was a large trade vessel and she was beautiful. Her figurehead was a lion leaping through waves, the lioness of the sea, the Ariela. He'd seen the ship and her captain, Bez Masudo, a few times before.

He walked up the quay, pausing near the ship, and waited. After a short time, a sailor noticed him. He was a big, burly, black-skinned, dark brown-eyed man of the Southern Islands with long braided black hair, his muscled shirtless chest covered in tattoos. The sailor pointed him out to the captain, who Bayani knew by reputation. Bez Masudo was an older man now, his long braided hair nearly half gray, but his tattoo-covered and tanned barrel-shaped body was still thick with the muscles of a sailor, and his brown eyes shone with intellect. Bayani took a deep breath as the two men approached him. "Greetings, Captain Masudo."

Captain Masudo nodded. "Weh mi can help yuh wid young man?"

"I wish to serve on your ship. I am Am'ayim, and I want to be a sailor."

The captain thumbed one of his earlobes, looking thoughtful. "Yuh a waan shore pikni? Fram Kinrai?"

"Yes, I was born here. I grew up in the streets and had to survive."

The burly sailor nodded and spat into the water. "Di streets dem a Kinrai a one hard place." He pointed at the two kali sticks on Bayani's back. "Yuh know how fi use dem deh?"

Bayani nodded with pride. "Yes, I do, old man Mataalii taught me."

The man nodded and looked at the captain. "Im a shore pikni, bot Kali a no likkle ting an di uol man a tof tiicha. Him remind mi a anodda shore pikni we did tek onboard once, not even Am'ayim, mi seh we gib im a chance."

Bayani had to hide his shock. A sailor who was not only a shore child but wasn't even Am'ayim aboard their ship? That must be an interesting story, and apparently, it meant he had chosen the right ship, too. He looked at the captain, who finally nodded. "Wi a go a Nordria next, yuh can sail wid wi an wi ago si how yuh do."

Bayani nodded. "Thank you, Captain."

The captain merely nodded while walking away. "Absai, put wi new bwoy to work."

Chapter Five:
Di Ariela
(Lioness of the Sea)

"Hindi lahat ng hangin ay mararamdaman.
Ang iba ay hangin ng tadhana.

Nuh all winds cyan no felt. Sum a di winds a fate.

Not all winds can be felt. Some are the winds of fate."

- Am'ayim Saying

Present day . . .

In port at Haversfjord, Absai leaned against the ship's railing, watching a specific young, red-haired lady saying goodbye to her two friends. He was more than a little annoyed at this whole situation. Their passenger looked like a pretty young thing he'd like to dandle on his knee, but she had the demeanor of a high lady and was supposed to be a

Weaver. These things just didn't connect the right way as far as he was concerned, but the captain had made their decision. It didn't help that he knew his old friend Bez was correct, either. He spat into the water as she left her friends and headed towards the ship, and even that was an odd display. When she parted from them, she looked like a young girl leaving her home and unsure about her future. She even stopped once to look back for a few moments. But by the time she reached the Ariela, her strides were long, her back straight, and she looked the perfect resemblance of a queen boarding her own vessel. They were in for a very long trip.

Palani came to stand by him, crossing his arms and nodding. "Yu no laik wi nyuu pasinja?"

Absai spat off the side again before answering. "Shi a waan difficult uman, demand dis an dat, knowing bout ka'u malihini taumatau, an act like Di Ariela a har ship."

Palani laughed. "Shi nuo likkle bout fi wi kolcha, dat a waan gud sitn mi fren."

Before Absai could reply, Rangi, who was walking by while carrying a rope with Fatiou, did instead. "Yuh jus upset cause shi pull yuh ova di mast pan har first day yah!" He closed his mouth and frowned, to which Fatiou laughed.

"A no jos dat!"

Fatiou laughed again and spoke to Rangi, but loud enough that he could hear. "Mi no tink im use to a likkle girl a boss him roun!" Both women laughed together at the joke, and Absai sighed. Women were all crazy.

Palani slapped him on the shoulder before walking away. "It a jos dem wie mi fren, aal uman mad."

Absai sighed and turned to watch as some of the Ariela's crew pushed her away from the dock with poles. Her sails had already been unfurled and the wind caught them as she slipped into the river's current. He got a brief chuckle out of watching the young lady stumble as the ship started moving, but that ended quickly a moment later, as something invisible like air seemed to catch her and she stood straight with no difficulty. Knowing what a Weaver could do was one thing, seeing it was more than a little unsettling. He didn't like this situation at all.

He watched her stalk across the ship like it belonged to her, straight to their other passengers. She seemed to take one look at the Danae woman and child with the different colored eyes before telling them in no uncertain terms that they were staying with her in the cabin. He smiled at the look on the Danae woman's face, but then she stopped to laugh and smiled before exclaiming that she liked the young lady. Absai sighed and turned to spit off the ship again but caught sight of Rangi and Fatiou looking at him, both highly amused. Palani was right; all women were crazy.

***

The Ariela slowly flowed into motion, as some of the dockhands used poles to push her away from the docks, and her sails caught the wind. The deck moved unsettlingly under Rosalie's feet, but she stood her ground, using Weaves of air to hold herself up. She watched her friends fade slowly away into the distance. She waved, hoping they could still see her. She would truly miss those two, especially Jonaas—how she wished for more time with him. She wiped her eyes and smiled. There was a new life ahead of her. It was time to go forward.

She turned to look around the ship. Sailors were running around everywhere, coiling ropes, loosening others, and doing all sorts of things she was not familiar with. The actual sailing of ships had never been high on her list for education. Across the deck, she saw the woman Jonaas had helped, huddling with her daughter in an out-of-the-way spot. They both looked so gaunt. The child was petting a very happy-looking orange ship's cat. "Mama, why does the ship have cats?"

Her mother smiled. "To help with the rats, sweetling."

They must not have had enough for more than passage. Jonaas could only afford to help so much, it seemed. Her mother's voice played in her mind. "Kindness is the true champion of greatness in us all . . ." She sighed and walked over to them, dodging around fast-moving barefoot sailors and trying not to fall as the ship moved. Sailing was not on her list of enjoyable activities.

She stopped near the two of them and looked down, only being startled for a brief moment by the young girl's different-colored eyes. "Come with me. The deck is no place for a woman and her child."

The woman looked up at her, surprised. "We didn't have enough for a cabin, but we're just staying out of the way. We have a hammock in the crew passageway. Thank you, but I couldn't."

Rosalie rolled her eyes and knelt down by them. She had to use more Weaves of air to not fall. Sailing! "A hammock is not enough room for the two of you and lacks privacy. You will gather yourself and come with me. You are a woman, not a sulking child, and I am helping both of you. On your feet." She stood and resisted the urge to snap her fingers like her mother used to.

The woman blinked, then laughed and started to stand up. "I think that I like you. Thank you, my name is Niomh, and this is Aife."

"I am Rosalie," she said while turning and heading toward the staircase leading to the ship's lower decks. Why were people so stubborn about accepting help when they needed it? She noted that the woman was more stable on her feet, too!

Captain Masudo looked at them quizzically when they reached him. "She will be staying with me. The crew passageway is no place for a woman and a child."

The captain nodded. "Yuh ago be crammed inna fish inna a barrel, but yuh can do as yuh please. It deh dung di ladder yah an straight ahead a yuh."

She nodded her thanks and headed down, not replying for fear she would say something wrong. He was easier to understand than the other sailor, but some words still escaped her. She used her hands to keep her balance instead of Weaving. Sometimes, it was good to do things with your own hands. Hopefully, the trip to Sceotan was short. The lower deck was lit by encased lanterns fastened to the walls. There were doors and openings everywhere, some of which housed cannons, but there was only one at the end of the hall straight ahead. The door was dimly lit by the lanterns and appeared to be just a touch larger than the others. She headed that way, her new traveling companions right behind her.

***

Niomh entered the ship's cabin, right behind Rosalie. It was small, lit by several wall lanterns but warmer than outside, and had two bunks. She didn't know what to think. Being away from her people had been so hard for so long. She'd gotten used to the cruelty of other people, and the Danae were gentle, kind-hearted people. Then that boy and this girl helped her for no apparent reason. She sat on the bunk near the door and put her daughter down next to her. Aife looked around and smiled up at her. "We get to stay here mama?"

She stroked her daughter's hair gently. "Yes, sweetling, we do, thanks to Rosalie. Get some rest now." Aife lay down next to her and curled up with one of their new blankets. Her daughter was excited to be on the ship, but she was also exhausted. No one slept much when living on the streets.

Niomh looked over at Rosalie, who was putting her satchel next to the other bunk, before sitting in the small chair with a book in her hand. "Why are you helping us?"

She looked up. "I am helping you because I can. My friend, Jonaas, has already helped you as well. I could not bear thinking of you and your daughter sleeping in the busy, cold crew passageway; it's no place for a woman and child."

Niomh blinked. Her friend? "The boy who gave us the blankets and food. Who paid for our journey? He is your friend?!"

Rosalie smiled, but something emotional passed across her face. "Jonaas. He has been my friend since we were children. He has the biggest heart I know."

What truly marvelous people. "Where are you from that made such kind folk out of you both?"

"A small farm town in Eastern Aedonia named Aliselle Falls. The woman who raised me was Jonaas' aunt. Her cabin was on their family's land, so Jonaas and I grew up together." She hesitated for a brief moment. "We were very close." That same emotion crossed Rosalie's face again.

Did she say Aedonian? "That is truly astounding. I've never seen such kindness from Aedonians before. Thank you so much."

Rosalie sighed and looked thoughtful. "I am sorry you experienced hardship at the hands of my people. Not all of us are like that, however. Where are you from?"

"I'm Danae. My people are nomadic, but many of us live in the southern parts of the Tanglewood, near Tursim, where the ship will be dropping us off. It's not far by ship. But we didn't have enough for passage and food."

Rosalie nodded. "I understand completely. Traveling is difficult. I am more than happy Jonaas and I could help you and your child. She is a beautiful little girl, especially with her strange eyes."

"Thank you. My people believe that children born with different-colored eyes have great destinies ahead of them. I'd given up on that before you and Jonaas." Niomh wiped her eyes, feeling that sadness again, but smiled. Looking at Rosalie, she suddenly knew what that emotion had been. "You loved him, didn't you?"

Rosalie met her eyes and gently closed her book. "I did. He was such a kind-hearted and intelligent man."

Niomh nodded, understanding. She'd seen as much in her brief encounter with Jonaas. "Why didn't he come with you?"

Rosalie stared out the cabin windows, lost in thought, as a tear trickled down her cheek. "Following a Weaver is not so simple. I would have eventually bonded him as my goddess bound, and Jonaas has always had a free spirit. I could not bear to take that away from him."

Niomh felt shocked. "You are a Weaver?!"

Rosalie nodded. "I can Weave. I will not officially be a Weaver until I complete my training on Sceotan. That is the purpose of my journey."

Niomh blinked, staring at Rosalie, who was still looking out the windows, lost in thought. "I've heard rumors and stories, but what is a goddess bound exactly?"

Rosalie replied calmly, as if reciting facts from memory that were easy for her. "Goddess bound are the sworn protectors and servants of a Weaver. The bond is forever and provides increased strength, healing, endurance, a longer life, and a sense of location. But it also makes the person likely to obey the Weaver's every wish."

Niomh nodded solemnly. "I understand why you couldn't bond him then. You are a truly wise young woman and just as kind for making that choice. You must have really loved him."

Rosalie didn't reply, and Niomh chose not to push the conversation. They had just met, and this was a sensitive subject. Instead, she lay down by her daughter and hugged her close before closing her eyes to rest.

Chapter Six:
Buhay ng Barko
(A Ship's Life)

"Ang isang barko ay buhay, tulad ng kanyang mga tauhan.

Waan ship alaiv, jus laik har kruu.

A ship is alive, just like her crew."

- Am'ayim Saying

Later that day, Rosalie walked out onto the deck and almost stumbled. She had to quickly weave a few threads of air to maintain her balance. Sailing was truly not for her, but she could not stay inside that small cabin forever, and her curiosity had gotten the best of her. Also, Niomh and her daughter were still sleeping. Their life was difficult, judging by what Rosalie had gathered. So it was either come up here or sit there pining over Jonaas, crying over Crilla, or pondering her difficult future. She took a deep breath and sighed, looking up at the sunny sky and feeling the wind in her hair. This would be a good day. It would!

Rosalie looked around the ship curiously. There were sailors everywhere, sweeping the deck with a sandy-looking material, pulling or releasing various ropes, or just sitting to coil or knot other ropes. She finally decided on a person to talk with, a young-looking Am'ayim woman who looked similar to the captain somehow. She was working by herself at the back of the ship.

She approached the woman cautiously, unsure if there was etiquette involved in talking with any of the crew. The woman was a few years older than Rosalie. She was well-muscled though still sinuously feminine. Her black hair was tightly braided in multiple rows along her head, and she had brown eyes. Like all of the other sailors, she was wearing no shoes or shirt. Her bare chest gleamed in the sun with sweat from her work, and she had quite a few tattoos.

Rosalie stopped nearby and observed what the woman was doing before speaking. It appeared as though she was wrapping string around a rope fastened to each side of the ship.

The woman looked over at her as if wondering what she wanted.

"Hello, I am Rosalie. Can I ask your name, and about what you are doing there? That looks like very hard work for a woman."

The woman was not rude exactly, but her voice took on the tone of someone who was very busy as she continued to wrap the string around the rope in a coil pattern. "Mi name Rangi, mi a worm di rope yah. Mi a Am'ayim, tu wi uman dem a di siem ting laik man. Hard or easy work nuh matta, wi do weh necessary."

Rangi was a little harder to understand than the captain, but thankfully still much better spoken than the big burly sailor. "Do the Am'ayim people truly value women that way? Is that why you are safe without a shirt among all the men aboard ship and why you are doing such hard work?"

Rangi laughed. "Aye, to di Am'ayim uman, dem very important an well respected." A look passed across her face as though she wanted to say more but she stopped speaking and continued her work.

"That is interesting! You called this worming?"

Rangi pointed at the rope right where she was about to wrap it in string. "Yuh si yah? Di hemp rope have contlines, dem a di spaces between strands a rope. Mi a wrap string inna dem lines yah, a di first step fi mek rope strong against di weather."

Rosalie watched closer for a few moments and indeed saw that Rangi was wrapping the string between the rope's strands. How interesting. "You said this was the first step? What else must you do?"

Rangi looked mildly annoyed but kept answering her question very politely. "Next mi haffi use tar, fram dat deh barrel deh, fi coat di rope." She pointed at a nearby barrel. "Den, afta di tar is only a likkle dry mi ago wrap di rope inna overlapping layers a thin canvas. Dis a wa dem call parceling." She glanced at Rosalie, making eye contact to make sure she was paying attention. She also noticed that the longer she paid attention and asked questions that showed she was listening, the more friendly Rangi became. "Afta dat mi ago coat di rope inna tar again, den wrap it inna twine, but wid di opposite coiling, dis a call serving. Finally a coat a tar, varnish, an paint."

Rosalie blinked. That was so much work for just a rope! She looked around the ship. There was rope everywhere. Did they have to do this for all of them? "Must you do this for every rope on the ship? That seems like so much hard work. Is it truly necessary?"

Rangi stopped for a moment, standing straight to stretch her back. Bending over rope all day would take a toll on anyone. "Aye, it is necessary fi any rope pan di ship weh nuh need flexibility. Di Saalt no kain tu rop an wi ship laif dipen pan dem."

"A ship's life?"

Rangi bent back over to start wrapping the rope again. "Aye, wi ship, Di Ariela. Shi alaiv, stap an lisn, fiil har." She knocked on the nearby railing with her knuckles, pulled gently on a rope hanging nearby, and then pointed at the sails. "Shi have bones, sinew, an shi always a move an a breathing."

Rosalie looked around the ship, considering Rangi's words. Alive? She closed her eyes and breathed. She could feel the ship moving on the river, hear the ropes creaking, feet thudding back and forth of barefoot sailors, wood groaning, and sails billowing. She opened her eyes, understanding. "Thank you, Rangi. I think I see what you mean. May I heal your back?" Rangi looked at her, confused, so Rosalie explained further. "It is something all Weavers can do with their power." She held out her hands. "If I may?"

Rangi shook her head. "Tank yuh, bot mi nuh need dat, aches an pain a part a Am'ayim laif."

Rosalie nodded and let it be. This is why she preferred to ask first. Not all people appreciated or even wanted a Weaver's power touching them. "Thank you, Rangi." She smiled before continuing to walk around the ship. A man was repairing pulleys ahead of her. She had seen them above holding the ship's ropes everywhere, so curious, she headed towards him.

***

Rangi glanced over as Bayani stopped near her and leaned against the ship's railing. He smiled when their eyes met, and she sharpened her gaze, knowing exactly what he was up to. He still had a lot to learn about the Masudo women. He just pretended not to notice her look and spoke anyway. Was he stubborn or unobservant? She wasn't sure, but he was handsome with his short black hair and light brown eyes, so she let him talk. "I'm done with my duties, I can help you with the ropes."

She didn't even look up. Assuming she needed help? Hopefully, he'd go away. "Yu a waan priti bwai, bot mi no niid yu elp."

Bayani just quietly got a small pail of tar and a rag and then started applying it where she had already wormed the rope. Rangi looked at him, ready to rake him over the deck, but he kept quietly working. She watched him for a few moments and noted he was doing a skillful job, so she let him keep doing it. That was definitely the only reason! She looked at him again. He looked up at just that moment, and their eyes met. He smiled and then went back to work. "Everyone can use a little help sometimes. It doesn't mean they're weak." He kept stolidly working. "In fact, it takes a certain kind of strength to accept and willingly work with others."

Rangi allowed herself to smile, just a little, definitely not enough that he would notice. "Mi si unu wid unu sinawali stik dem, unu nuo ou fi yuuz dem?"

He kept applying tar without looking up as he replied. "You did good work worming this. Yes, I know how to use the sticks. I trained under Old Mataalii in Kinrai. You were very patient with our young Weaver guest."

Rangi was almost done working this segment of rope, which was good because her fingers were sore. This minute and delicate fingerwork was still new to her. "Har name is Rosalie, a uman who will be called by har name. Shi is very curious, pay attention, and ask good kweschans." She looked across the deck for a moment and laughed. Rosalie was apparently bothering Tane about rigging pulleys now.

Bayani also looked and chuckled quietly. "I think she will be like this for the entire journey. Inquisitive minds don't rest easy."

Rangi finished her work and stood up to stretch her back and arms again. She looked at Bayani and realized he was almost done tarring the rope for this coating. It would need a bit of time to dry before they could parcel it, and it had been a while since she'd been able to hit someone. She flexed her hands, then clenched her fists and smiled. "Wen yu don wid dat de priti bwai mi waan si ou yu kyaa yu stik dem."

He looked up at her and smiled. There was a gleam in his eyes. "That sounds like a great idea."

***

"How often do you have to swab the entire deck?" Rosalie was talking to Akua, the ship's cabin boy. He did not have any earrings yet. She had just learned from Maleko a little bit ago that the number of earrings an Am'ayim sailor wore denoted their rank. They had such an interesting culture. The ship suddenly rolled in a fashion that did not agree with Rosalie's footing, and she had to use Weaves of air to hold herself up. Sailing was definitely a less-than-enjoyable endeavor.

Akua looked over at her. He was much younger than the other crew members and, though busy, did not seem to mind talking with her. Maybe it was a nice break from his hard work. "Mi haffi swab di deck every day, more sometimes."

Thankfully, Akua was learning from the more well-spoken crew members. "Every day? That must be very hard work, especially when you are still so young. You are such a good worker."

He smiled as the sun glinted off his brown eyes, which had turned amber in the sunlight. His big smile was way too pretty for such a young man; he was going to be a heartbreaker one day. "Tank yuh Weaver." Then they both turned because they heard a commotion across the deck.

There was a small group of crew surrounding two people who were circling one another. It was Rangi and a young Am'ayim man she did not know. They were circling each other in a small space, surrounded by a group of other sailors. Rosalie heard bets being laid, crude jokes, laughing, and taunts. Curious, she went to watch. Unfortunately, most of the crude jokes and taunts stopped when she got close. She had always found the ones used by farm hands back home interesting. It would have been nice to hear these as well.

Rangi was holding her arms up, with closed fists, in some sort of fighting stance, circling her opponent with swift, surefooted leg movements. The young man had two short sticks held in front of him to strike and guard, but his legs moved in a similar fashion. He moved in to strike with his sticks, but Rangi seemed to flow around him as she sidestepped his blows, swept his legs, and hit him square in the face with her fist as he fell. The small group of sailors all started laughing as marks exchanged hands, and a few forgot themselves enough to say a few of those jokes, though Rosalie was not sure what a sea cow was or how beating one with a jellyfish had anything to do with fighting. She also did not understand why these two were fighting in the first place.

But then Bez stormed into the small group, stomping and yelling. He was quite impressive when he needed to be. Somehow, he reminded her of Gertrude when the boys were misbehaving back home. "Weh unu sail strapped idiots a duh!?" He looked at Rangi and pointed at her. "Yu shuda nuo betta!" She looked down in shame as another sailor helped the young man up, and the group dispersed. Bez grabbed the young man by his shoulder and looked him in the eyes. "Bayani! Yuh deh pan di night shift fi dis, maybe next time yuh wi tink betta."

Bayani nodded, looking a bit chastised and rubbed his heavily bruised cheek. "Yes, Captain."

Bez looked back at Rangi again. "Back to yuh ropes. Mi disappointed." After everyone else had left their vicinity he looked at Rosalie. "Please pardon mi kruu Weaver. Dem shuda nuo betta."

"Why were they fighting?"

Bez laughed. "Dem did jus a have a likkle fun, but wen wi deh a sail dem shuda nuo betta. Pan lan mi woulda be joining in an betting, too."

Rosalie blinked in mild astonishment. They had been actually fighting for fun, not sparring in a friendly manner. The Am'ayim were going to take some getting used to! "Thank you, Captain. I believe that it is time for me to get some rest."

CHAPTER SEVEN: NIOMH AND AIFE

"The Danae are among the most open-hearted and kind people in Innatraea. This is both their strength and their downfall."

- Tavid the Traveler

Niomh looked up from the chair she was sitting in as Rosalie entered the cabin. "That was quite the ruckus we heard from above."

"Two of the crew were fighting one another. Just for the fun of it, apparently! The Am'ayim and their speech will take some getting used to."

"They are a very interesting people, kinder than most, especially where women are concerned, but they do believe in violence. And yes, their accent is very interesting."

Aife looked at them from their bunk, where she was eating and petting one of the ship's cats. "They do talk funny. I thought violence was wrong, Mama?"

Niomh looked at her daughter and smiled. "It is wrong, sweetling, but Innatraea is not that simple. Different people look at what is right and wrong in different ways. That is also true for speech as every place has different accents and languages." Aife took on a look of concentration but soon got distracted by eating her food and playing with the orange ship's cat.

Rosalie sat in the other chair and wisely chose not to butt into that conversation but instead to move on to another topic. "I see there is food. I am famished."

Niomh had already gotten food for them since she'd woken up and seen that Rosalie was out. Nikau, the ship's chef, had been more than willing to have his helper Salesi give her enough for the three of them, though it was still only salted beef, biscuits, pears, cheese, and a strong black tea called assam the Am'ayim preferred. Aife was already happily eating and sharing with one of the ship's cats, which was both unfortunate and adorable. "I got food for you. I think Nikau is also making some sort of gruel for everyone tonight."

Rosalie wrinkled her nose. "Gruel? Goddess no! Thank you for thinking of me. I appreciate it." She picked up the tea kettle and very carefully poured herself half a mug, as there were no normal teacups aboard. Then she inhaled the steam coming off her mug and smiled. "This actually smells good, though strong." She took a sip.

Niomh poured herself some more tea as well and sipped it cautiously, then coughed. "That is indeed quite strong."

Aife looked over laughing. "It's good to dip biscuits in! But the cat doesn't like it. He just wants salted beef!"

Rosalie smiled as she mixed cheese and pears for dinner. "All animals love salt. We used to hide it back home so they would not eat it all."

Aife looked over. "Really? Even the cows and horses?"

"Even the cows and horses. The barn cats were the worst, though, because they could climb and were smarter than the others. They always found it."

Aife laughed and went back to eating while sharing with the cat. "Do you think he finds food they hide on the ship?"

Niomh smiled at her daughter. "I'm sure he does. You'll have to ask Nikau."

Rosalie smiled mischievously. "Aife, after dinner, I have something that I need your help with."

Niomh raised her eyebrow at her, but Aife replied first. "What is it!?"

Rosalie paused, holding a piece of biscuit in her hand. "You will have to finish your dinner to find out," she said.

Aife started eating faster, and Niomh chuckled quietly to herself. "You're quite good with children."

"Children are so pure and honest. They always love to try new things and are incredibly inquisitive. I love them."

"Do you plan on having your own someday?"

Rosalie sighed. "It is a bit more complicated for a Weaver. We can still have children, but there is no guarantee that they will inherit our ability to weave." She looked down at the teacup in her hands and thought, *It is already hard enough knowing I will outlive my friends. I do not know if I could stand to outlive my child.* Rosalie closed her eyes quietly for a few moments.

"I am sorry. I understand. That must be difficult. I can't imagine having to make such choices." She watched Rosalie for a moment. The young woman was such a strong person for her age; she was truly remarkable.

Then Aife started jumping up and down excitedly, much to the dismay of the orange ship's cat, which moved to the other bunk. "What did you need my help with?"

Rosalie opened her eyes and smiled. Then a bright sphere-shaped yellow light appeared in the air next to her. "This is a glow orb. All Weavers can make them. They are made of light and can be in any color and many different sizes." It floated over towards Aife. "Here, have a look."

Niomh smiled as her daughter looked at the thing curiously and poked it with her finger. "I can't touch it!"

Rosalie nodded. "That is correct. They are made out of light. Now look." The glow orb split apart into about a dozen smaller ones, about marble-sized, and in various colors. They floated around Aife, who started laughing and jumping around, trying to catch them. "Now I have an idea: we could make different shapes by putting glow orbs together. Do you want to help me? What shape could we make?"

Niomh leaned back in her chair and sighed, happily watching her daughter as Aife stopped jumping and tapped her chin thoughtfully. "Can we make a cat?"

Rosalie nodded. "Sure, but we may need more glow orbs for that." Another dozen or so small marble-sized lights appeared and slowly floated near each other in the shape of a cat. "How is this?"

Aife looked at it closely, giggling. "It's so funny-looking!" She pointed at one of its legs and started laughing. "This leg is shorter than the others!"

Rosalie smiled and nodded. "Yes, it is! I apparently need some practice making animals. This is what I needed your help with." One more small glow orb appeared and floated into place on the shorter leg.

Aife was obviously more than happy to help. "Let's make a fish next!"

Niomh smiled, watching her daughter play with Rosalie and the glow orbs. She'd never imagined seeing her little Aife this happy a few days ago. Then that boy had given them hope, and now his friend, who just happened to be a Weaver, was taking care of them on their voyage. She wanted to cry from happiness, it was unbelievable. She took a sip of her tea, then set it carefully aside and picked up the book Rosalie had put down. The cover said *Amah: The Morals of the Weave.*

Later, after Aife had finally fallen asleep and Niomh was tucking her into their bunk, Rosalie looked over at her. "Aife certainly ate a lot of food for a little girl, hopefully she will start looking healthier soon."

Niomh smiled fondly while gently stroking her sleeping daughter's hair. "I hope so too, thank you. She's still not used to having food available."

Rosalie nodded. "That is highly unfortunate, but it makes sense. Hopefully, that will change with time. You never told me what happened to you two. How did you end up on the streets of Haversfjord like that?"

Niomh sat down on the bunk next to Aife with her own blanket and met Rosalie's eyes. "It's hard to admit, but I am to blame for that. I fell for the wrong man and left home with him. When Aife was born, he left us to fend for ourselves." She felt tears again just thinking about it. She loved her daughter, but the event that had led to Aife's birth was the biggest mistake she had ever made, and it still hurt. "My people have a phrase for what both Aife and I went through. The journey of sorrow."

Rosalie met her eyes and nodded, smiling compassionately, but her latent curiosity remained. "Journey of sorrow? That sounds incredibly sad. What does it mean?"

Niomh wiped her eyes before closing them and leaning her head down. She could feel the tears of shame and sadness flowing down her cheeks. "It is when one of our people leaves home, then returns much later, after the outside world breaks their heart." She opened her eyes, still crying quietly, and laid her hand on Aife's sleeping form. "The Danae are very gentle and kind-hearted people. Many never make it back home after that..."

Rosalie came to stand by Niomh and hugged her. "I am sorry you experienced that. I cannot claim to understand, but I think you will both be all right now. Sometimes, the Three Sisters work in mysterious ways."

Niomh let the younger woman hold her as she cried, unable to remember the last time she felt safe enough to do that.

CHAPTER EIGHT:
SEME ANDO BALVAL
(SEEDS IN THE WIND)

Rosalie walked out onto the deck to a sunny yet chilly morning, especially with the river's brisk wind. She was used to it; they were now a week or more into the journey. Being on the water was almost like being in a different world in so many ways. She walked to the railing and watched the shore flowing by. They were passing by what looked like rocky hills, with the occasional high pass and clumps of unruly trees. She had been told that the vast plains many called The Sea of Grass were beyond these hills, but she unfortunately couldn't see it. Truthfully, she had no idea where they were aside from still being on the Victory River. A few days ago they passed a fort town, which Bez had said was called Feorrker; they hadn't stopped though, because apparently the Holy

Church of Jhoras controlled that town. She shivered, partly due to the cold morning air but also because of her thoughts about the Jhorians. She made a small nimbus of flame in the air near her, which helped.

Rosalie looked over as one of the crew came to stand nearby. "Dat a quite di trick, di wind nuh even put di flame out! A Weaver being aboard a very interestin."

Rosalie smiled at him. He was relatively easy to understand, and she had been getting more used to their strange dialect. "Good morning. It is quite chilly on the Victory in the mornings. I do not believe we have met yet."

The man nodded. "Mi name a Atawhai. Di flame very useful, plenty Am'ayim woulda pay fi dat deh trick. Yahso dem call di riva Nehri Zengin, it means riva a wealth."

Rosalie laughed. "Here, you can borrow this one for free." She created the same for him, too, and he smiled appreciatively while warming his hands on it. "Why does the river have a different name here?"

"Evri piipl, dem niem tingz fi dem uona miinin. All a Innatraea a like dat." He stepped up to the railing, resting his hands on it and watched the shore flowing by with her. "But di riva? Shi no kier, so shi ron we shi waan, an wi siel har."

"That is very interesting and makes so much sense. Thank you for sharing. It must be amazing to see all of Innatraea while sailing." Rosalie took a deep breath, enjoying the morning and conversation. "Your people have such interesting names, too, Atawhai. Do they have different meanings to them?"

He nodded. "Dem mean plenty different tings. To Am'ayim, a name is important. Mi name mean kind an caring. A gud Am'ayim always try fi live up to dem name inna life. A wi way."

"I understand. That is marvelous. Where I come from, names are not as important. It is just what we are known by. I am very impressed by your people's culture."

He nodded. "Tank yuh Weaver, a jus wi way."

The Am'ayim had such an interesting mix of perspectives. In some ways, they were very humble, yet in others, they possessed a unique bravado she had never seen before. She was beginning to hope that the journey would take a little longer so she could get to know their people better. She still had not even met half of the crew! She was about to ask Atawhai more about Am'ayim names when they both heard a loud yell from above and turned to look.

Rosalie saw a sailor falling off the high center mast of the ship and started weaving to catch him immediately, even if he was the burly, crude, and annoying sailor she had met first, Absai. That was no reason to let him get hurt when she could easily prevent it. Oddly, another sailor whose name she thought was Amari was just below him on the mast and started climbing down after he saw Absai begin slowly floating to the deck. They must have been racing one another. Dangerous fool stunts were normal amongst their people she was finding. Rosalie dropped him the last couple of feet just to show him what she thought about his behavior. The thump and his loud yelp were both quite satisfying indeed.

Bez stopped near her, laughing so hard he had to bend over. "Dat a tiich yu waan lesn, fuul!"

Amari dropped the last few feet and landed on the deck just as Absai was getting up. He was also laughing. "Yu siev im an tiich im waan lesn!"

Absai flexed his right arm a bit, obviously in pain, but did not complain about it. He did, however, look more than mildly chastised. "Tank yuh, Weaver." He pointedly did not meet her eyes.

Bez started speaking just before she offered to heal Absai's arm. "Dat a-go tiich unu fuul-fuul piipl se unu no fi ron op di mast dem laik manki! Jus be glad di young Weaver did deh yah fi help. Now, get bak a work!"

Rosalie carefully lowered her hand and kept silent. Being Am'ayim was one thing. But racing up the mast of a moving ship . . . why would anyone in their right mind do that? Absai could enjoy his sore arm and be glad that was all he had gotten! She turned to head down to her cabin. Niomh and Aife should be up soon, and they could all have breakfast together.

But Bez stopped her. "Please walk wid mi a moment, Weaver."

He was oddly calmer and more reasonable than the other sailors. Maybe it was because he was older? She stepped in beside him as he started walking the deck. "Certainly, Captain, what can I do for you?"

"Tank yuh fi save Absai, im a waan gud sailor but im can be a brash fuul." He stopped to inspect the knots holding a rope and nodded.

"Of course, it is the least I can do. I would not allow anyone serious harm when I can easily prevent it."

She had seen him do this before, walking the ship and checking random things everywhere. "Yuh a waan gud sumady, not all Weavers mi meet a kind. Most a yuh kind wouldn't tek on a destitute mada har pikni wid strange eyes, or help mi kruu."

"I am sorry to hear you have had negative experiences with Weavers. I am not, however, quite yet one of them. I am going there to train. That is my purpose currently."

He stopped to watch the sails and rigging for a moment. There always seemed to be sailors everywhere on the rigging doing some small thing, and this was no exception. "Mi surprised. Yuh carry yuhself well, fi such a young lady."

She looked down for a moment, not used to such compliments. "Thank you, Captain. I appreciate your kind words. Why do you mention Aife's eyes as though they matter to you?"

Bez chuckled quietly while cinching a nearby knot. "Am'ayim believe seh different colored eyes a waan sign a fate, dis can be gud or bad. All a mi kruu don note har eyes."

Rosalie nodded. The explanation made sense, as many different cultures had superstitions about such things, even Niomh's own people, the Danae. "Thank you, Captain. Now, what did you really want of me this morning?"

He eyed her shrewdly. "Yuh smart as well, mi have a favor fi ask if yuh. Wen yuh a ask kweschan, please stay wid di off duty kruu, Di Ariela a waan busy ship an dat woulda help mi."

She paused for a moment in thought. Of course, the request made sense. She could recall how busy everyone had always been whenever she asked them about what they were doing. She suddenly felt horrible about it but tried not to show it because she could remember Crilla's words. *A Weaver must always appear certain . . .*

"Of course, Captain, my apologies. How long until we reach Sceotan?"

"Turism, weh wi ago stop fi trade fi a few days, is bout a week away. Afta dat wi ago head across di ocean fi Sceotan, maybe waan month."

Rosalie smiled. "Thank you, Captain. I shall endeavor to bother the crew less."

He nodded. That was more than enough for him. He was a man of his word and expected no less of anyone aboard his ship. She watched him continue his rounds. He was almost like the ship's father, checking up on everyone, stern but caring and sure that he was ultimately in charge. She liked Bez Masudo; he was a good man. Her stomach rumbled, and she decided to go see if Niomh and Aife were up yet. It was time for breakfast.

***

Niomh barely caught their tray of food from tipping over as she walked onto the ship's deck. Aife darted away from her, having caught sight of Rosalie coming towards them. "Auntie Rosalie!"

Niomh's breath caught when she heard her daughter. Aife was still young and didn't know any better. She was just excited and adjusting to all the changes in their lives recently. But she didn't have to worry because Rosalie knelt and embraced Aife. "Good morning, little one. I see you are up and ready for adventure today." She looked at Niomh. Their eyes met for a brief moment before she looked back at Aife. "Remember, though, whenever you are on the ship's deck, stay close to your mother or myself. All right?"

Aife looked down in disappointment. "I'm sorry, I didn't mean to."

Rosalie just ruffled her hair and smiled again, though. "That is all right, little one. All of us learn by making mistakes. There is no need to apologize." She stood up and took Aife's hand. "It looks like your mother had an excellent idea. I think breakfast outside would be wonderful. We should go find an out-of-the-way spot."

Niomh carefully followed the two of them while trying to stay out of the sailors' way and balancing their tray of food. She had to smile, though, watching her daughter and Rosalie together. It was amazing how close they'd become so quickly. That is what happened when a person saved your life, took care of you, and you lived in close proximity for days. The two of them found a small space on the quarter deck. Her daughter was laughing and smiling. Niomh had never imagined seeing her little Aife that way. Rosalie was truly marvelous with children.

She truly hoped the young woman would have children of her own someday, though it wasn't that simple, and she understood that all too well. Niomh's journey of sorrow had taught her the power of seemingly small choices in life. What it must be like to have the power of a Weaver and still be a young woman, she didn't envy Rosalie that difficulty. It was good they were together, even for this short trip, because a woman like that needed friends. Something nibbled at the back of her mind as she reached the two, and Aife looked up at her, smiling with joy. Her daughter's different-colored eyes seemed to shine in the morning sunlight. *Great destinies . . .* A phrase she had heard once back home echoed that thought.

Seme ando Balval, or Seeds in the Wind. The Danae believed that destiny and fate moved an Innatraean to where they belonged, even through cruel hardship. But she shook off the thought and sat down with their food while trying to focus on what mattered now: the present and her daughter, who would be all right now. But she couldn't help but wonder what destiny awaited her little girl.

CHAPTER NINE: STAAM (STORM)

"Hindi lahat ng bagyo ay simpleng uri ng hangin at ulan.

Nuh all staams a di simple kain a breeze an rain.

Not all storms are the simple kind of wind and rain."

- Am'ayim Saying

A few days later, Fatiou looked up into the sky and scowled. The air felt different than it had when they'd set sail this morning. The wind was picking up and there were dark clouds in the distance. There was a storm coming right for them, and the river didn't give them the ability to run from it. It was bad luck to have a storm this soon into a new journey and even worse luck for that storm to catch them in the narrow waterway. If she remembered correctly, there was a cove not far from them. She saw Bez across the ship from her and went to him. "Kyapten?"

He stepped up beside her and lifted his spyglass to the horizon. "Kaka faat! Aye, mi see it. Wi have a storm a come."

"Di nearby cove?"

He nodded, lowering his spyglass. "Aye, mi ago mek di kruu change course. Wake everybody else."

"Kyapten? Di young Weaver an di pikni wid different colored eyes? Yuh tink wi fates dem woven?"

Bez laughed. "Dat a old seaman's nonsense, even if true, we have work fi do!!"

She nodded, touching her fingers to her lips. "Aye, Kyapten! I a go wake di kruu." He only nodded in response, already stomping off to issue orders. The captain of any ship was a spectacle, and Bez Masudo was no exception.

Fatiou went down the ladder to the crew passageway, where she found Absai trying to sleep in his hammock. "A time fi wake up! Ah staam a come!"

He swung his legs out of the hammock and stood immediately. He probably felt the ship turning or the waves changing slightly; he'd been a sailor for a long time. "Rasshole, mi awake. Wi did find a safe place fi weather har?"

She nodded, smiling. South Islanders liked to talk differently. She was glad another one was aboard with her. "Aye, yuh octopus pum pum, di kyapten a routing har to a nearby cove."

Absai nodded and yelled down the passageway. "Wake up all yuh lazy kakavlaats! Maleko! Kai! Unu two stay dung an batten everyting up!" They both went to work without a word. Good sailors knew their trade. "Fatiou, get di dinghies ready!"

She nodded and headed above deck. The storm didn't look bad, but it was best to be prepared. She heard Absai approaching right behind her and already issuing orders on his way to join the captain. But they were for others—she had her task already. Though preparing the dinghies wasn't hard, it just involved loosening some of their ropes so they could be released quickly in an emergency and making sure the nearby boarding ladders were ready. While she was doing this, Fatiou felt the Ariela start changing course and slowing down.

The cove came slowly into view. It was small and hidden by a treed rocky ridge until you were almost on top of it. But they often came this way and knew where it was. Thankfully, there hadn't been any other ships in the last few days, so they could maneuver into the cove freely. It was a tight course. She finished with the dinghies and ladders and joined the oarsmen. They would help guide the ship while entering the cove after the turn.

***

Rosalie looked up from her book. The ship had started slowing down and turning. She could feel the motion in her body. This was unexpected, as they were still almost a week from Tursim, according to her conversation with the captain several days ago. She also heard sailors running around and yelling above. Obviously, something was happening. Hopefully, whatever that something was, it was easily manageable. She did not believe in being ill-informed, however, so she decided to go have a look.

She had not really been reading anyway, just staring vacantly at the pages, remembering Crilla and wishing Jonaas was here.

Rosalie looked over at Niomh and Aife. Both were sleeping, which was something they'd been doing a lot of since coming aboard. Having a safe place to sleep was probably new to them. She put her book down and got up to go see what was happening. Her glow orb followed her as she opened the door to her cabin, and the orange ship's cat ran inside. Apparently, it did not appreciate whatever was happening above. She laughed and headed down the dimly lit passageway, her glow orb proving useful as the ship's lanterns only did so much to light the way.

Two sailors ran up and down the passageway, closed hatches and doors, and ensured everything was secure. Rosalie had to be careful in dodging out of their way so as not to lose her footing. The ship may not have been moving fast, but it still swayed in the river unsettlingly. Sailing was awful. She took a deep breath, and Crilla's words echoed in her mind: *A Weaver must always take charge of any given situation, especially a crisis . . .*

Rosalie floated her glow orb directly in front of one of the sailors' eyes, a man she recognized as Maleko. As he tried to run by her, he stopped, staring. "What is happening?"

He gulped nervously before replying. "A storm a come Weaver, wi a ready di ship."

She nodded and moved her glow orb out of his way, even though he could walk right through it. "Thank you, off with you."

He looked at her quizzically, unsure about being ordered about by a girl most likely, but he scurried away to follow whatever orders he had from his captain. Crilla told her that people were always odd when someone they did not expect took charge. She found seeing the behavior both slightly amusing and encouraging. Rosalie smiled and headed above to evaluate the situation for herself. *True courage is a matter of decisive intelligence as much as bravery . . .*

Rosalie stepped out onto the deck into heavy rain and wind. She expanded her glow orb into a flat disc, made it solid and floated it above herself. Truthfully, it did not help much with the wind, but it was better than nothing. Looking around, she located the captain and headed carefully in his direction. He was standing next to one of the strange-looking crew members, whom she had not yet had the chance to talk with. The person was wearing a robe, but it was sleeveless, revealing heavily tattooed muscular arms. They also had long, tightly braided hair and a big bushy beard. Finally, they were wearing necklaces made from what looked like animal bones.

She approached Bez as the ship slowed to a stop, and sailors dropped her anchor. "Captain, will the storm be a serious one?"

***

Masina looked at the young Weaver out of the corner of their eye as she joined them and addressed the captain. They noticed the clear disc-like thing above her blocking the rain, but neither mentioned it. Her abilities as a Weaver were well-known amongst the crew.

Bez looked over at her, while sparing the occasional eye for the crew, as was his captain's duty. "Di staam no luk bad, bot wi de nier Di Saalt an di briiz shif faas."

"Is that why we are sheltering in a cove?"

Bez only nodded, so Masina answered instead. "Aye, sheltering fi a storm is wise, especially close to Di Saalt. Mi ago mek an offer to Caim tu."

Her keen look of interest made Masina wish they hadn't spoken. "Tell me more about this offering and Caim." Her words had not been a request.

Bez nodded. "Mi lef yuh inna Masina's skilled hans Weaver, mi hab nuff fi do." He walked away.

Masina looked to make sure the young Weaver was paying attention, and then they pointed out into the water. "Di Saalt a Caim's realm, him a di god a death, weh drown di Am'ayim dem weh weak inna soul, body, a mind."

The Young Weaver looked out into the water for a moment and then back at them. "How does one prove their strength to Caim?"

"Wi Am'ayim du dis fram wi baan. Evri pikni baan iina Di Saalt, eni pikni we tuu wiik fi dat no sovaiv. Pikni dem weh baan pan lan dem niem shore pikni an weaker." He looked at her and nodded, seeing she was paying attention. "Wen wi face death wi challenge Caim, if wi survive wi tattoo dis pain pan wi skin." Masina indicated the tattoos on their arms.

Rosalie touched her chin thoughtfully, now completely ignoring the rain. "What an interesting belief system. It accounts for life, death, and hardship and celebrates survival. How do you make an offering for Caim now, for this storm?"

They laughed. "Yuh ask nuff kweschans Weaver. Mi a go do di offering now, watch if yuh waan."

Chapter Ten: Mga sipi (Passages)

"Ang mga daluyan ng tubig ng puso ay
kung saan ipinanganak ang katotohanan.

Di haat's wata ways a weh chuut baan.

The heart's waterways are where truth is born."

- Am'ayim Saying

Rosalie watched curiously as Masina reached into one of their many belt pouches and removed a handful of a white mineral-looking substance. "Is that salt?"

Masina nodded affirmatively and did not reply further. She supposed all her questions were probably a bother. Then they spoke in a different language—not the Am'ayim accented common she was used to—while throwing the salt out into the river. "Atua Caim whakaae tamiti pule onole wai."

They walked further down the ship to repeat the same actions and words. That was interesting. Maybe they had to bless the whole ship? Rosalie sighed. Much as she wanted to watch the whole ritual, she had to go and let Niomh know what was happening. She looked at the sky. It was starting to rain harder, and the wind was picking up. Being inside would be nice as well.

Rosalie turned and started walking back towards the ladder. The ship seemed to move even more under the increasing wind. She was finding it harder to keep her feet. So, she formed a small weave of air around herself to make things easier. A sailor came running out of the door as Rosalie neared. She thought his name was Kai, though they had not talked yet. She moved out of the way, and he ran by, noting that he was barefoot and did not slip a bit, even though the deck was soaking wet and the ship was moving. The different lives people lived were certainly interesting. She went down the ladder and headed towards her cabin but stopped at the small galley first.

The ship shifted under her feet again, but down here, there were walls, so she just used her hands, rather than her power, to catch herself. The ship's cook was inside the small galley. He looked up as she entered. "Deh have salted beef, cheese an pears fi now Weaver. Mi ago cook more afta di storm pass."

Rosalie nodded. "Thank you, Nikau. I shall take enough for the three of us. We will most likely be in our cabin until the storm passes." He nodded, and she took the food he handed her along with a knife, stacking it all in her arms. Then she continued on her way, noting that the second ship's cat, the gray and black one, was already outside her cabin.

Rosalie went inside, followed by the cat, and closed the door. Then she caught herself as the ship tilted again in the wind. Her power kept their food from falling. Niomh and Aife were both awake now. The girl was happily petting the orange cat, which was apparently of great interest to the gray and black one. "Mama, I'm glad the ship has rats!"

Niomh laughed. "Why would you be glad the ship has rats?" She looked up at Rosalie, a twinkle of humor in her eye.

Aife giggled happily and hugged the orange cat. "Because that's why they have cats!"

Rosalie smiled, too. Children were a wonder. "There is a storm coming in, that is why we have stopped. The captain says that, as of now, it should not be a bad one. It is probably best if we all just stay down here. I got food for us."

"Thank you. I was just going to go check the galley myself, but Aife woke up." She ruffled her daughter's hair. "You're too kind."

Rosalie handed her some food and the small knife, before sitting on her bunk. "Crilla always told me that everyone deserves kindness. If you have the power to help you always should."

Niomh looked over from handing her daughter a slice of pear with cheese. "Crilla? She sounds like a wise woman."

Rosalie smiled sadly and felt tears in her eyes. "She was one of the best people I ever knew. Kind, wise, and intelligent. She raised me after I was abandoned by my parents." Niomh met her eyes and nodded. The woman understood such things as abandonment, heartache, love, and loss without words.

***

Aife tried to grab the glowing elephant again and fell back on the bunk, laughing. The cats both looked at her, annoyed because she'd woken them up, so she petted them. The elephant split up into all the little glowing balls of light and swam around her again. She almost thought she could see little threads inside the small balls of light, but then they were gone, so she jumped up, trying to catch one, but they were always too fast for her. "Make a fairy again, Auntie Rosalie!"

Rosalie smiled and twirled her fingers around a little. The small balls of light became little faeries of different colors. "What about a lot of little faeries?"

Aife started clapping. No one had ever played with her like this before, and she knew she and her mama were safe here. Aife looked at her mama. She was relaxing in a chair and reading a book. She'd never seen her mama read before. "I love them!"

The cats had woken up and were watching the little faeries, too. A few floated near them, and they started swatting at them to no avail. Aife sat down and petted them again. "Mama, can we get a cat when we're back home?"

Her mama looked up and put a finger to mark her spot in the book. "Our people do have cats and dogs. Animals have spirits too and are important to us."

"I'm excited to see our people." She hugged the orange cat, which was nicer than the other one, and it started purring. "Will we be safe there and have a place to sleep?"

The faeries faded away as her mama closed the book, came to sit by her, and stroked her hair gently. "Yes, sweetling, they're our people. We will have our own place to sleep, be safe, and we can get a cat."

Aife lay in her mama's lap, suddenly feeling tired. "That's good."

She didn't see Rosalie and Niomh's eyes meet with that look women knew—one of both happiness and sadness. She was happy that they would be safe amongst their people again, but she was sad that such a young child as Aife had to worry about being safe.

***

"Aife really is a wonderful child. You have done well with her, given the situation you were both in."

Niomh looked over from her place on their bunk and smiled. "Thank you. Truthfully, I don't even know how I managed. Raising a child without your family or a home is impossible."

Rosalie smiled from her bunk where she was sitting while petting the gray and black ship's cat. "Yet you have done well."

Niomh smiled now too. "Thank you. That means a lot coming from someone like you."

"Will you truly have a safe place to live once you are back with your people?"

"Yes, we are a communal people. It's not like most places. All Danae have safety, shelter, and food when they're amongst our people's caravans."

"That is very interesting. I do not think that I have ever heard of people like that before. How is everything paid for?"

73

Niomh laughed. "We don't have the same system of money as other places. We all just live and work for what we need. What little is necessary, we trade for with others."

"That is truly remarkable. I would like to visit your people and see them for myself after my training is complete."

Niomh brushed a single tear from her cheek. "You would always be welcome there. I don't think we will ever be able to repay the debt we owe you and your friend Jonaas for helping us. I don't think we would have made it without you two."

"Jonaas has always been like that. Truthfully, I am just happy you are both here. Having you and Aife near me has made this journey much easier than it would have been alone."

Niomh smiled at Rosalie's awkward tone. She wasn't very good at taking compliments or admitting she needed someone else. "Traveling with you has been a pleasure. Aife has been happier than I have ever seen her."

"I am more than happy to give that wonderful girl a fighting chance. I feel an affinity towards her." She looked at Aife's sleeping form and smiled warmly.

Niomh eyed Rosalie coyly. "Is that your way of saying that you love my daughter?"

Rosalie laughed softly. "I suppose that is exactly right. Jonaas was easy for me. We grew up together and knew one another better than anyone else. Other people, I do not have as easy a time understanding."

"Really? You seem just fine with the Am'ayim, myself, and Aife."

Rosalie looked thoughtful. "That is true. However, I have apparently been a bother to many of the sailors with my questions. The captain even felt as though he had to say something. Perhaps there is a difference between those I am comfortable with and those I am not. I shall have to pay closer attention to that."

Niomh smiled. She had forgotten just how young Rosalie actually was and that she had grown up in a small farm village. Even though the young Weaver was incredibly intelligent and powerful, certain things just had to be learned with experience. "You are thinking about it too much. It's as simple as the sailors being very different from your home, and you, having rescued us, makes us closer to you."

Rosalie nodded. "You are quite right. Some things are just that simple. I never had to deal with so many people back home. It was just those I had known my whole life and Crilla's education on the Weavers."

"I think you will do fine. Just remember that everyone is inherently another Innatraean and treat them the same. Your heart is a good one, they'll see it."

Rosalie hung her dress up. "Thank you, Niomh, you have been a good friend to me."

Niomh lay down next to her daughter, covering herself with their blankets, too. She couldn't remember the last time they'd been in a place where she could sleep safely. She looked over at Rosalie. Their eyes met briefly, and Niomh smiled warmly before closing hers. Did Rosalie truly understand just how miraculous her and Jonaas' intervention had been? She hugged her daughter and fought off her silent tears before snuggling Aife close to sleep. Without them, her little Aife might not be here anymore. That was a kindness she could never forget.

CHAPTER ELEVEN:
SA DILIM (IN THE DARK)

"Je maha nga mea e huna ana e te po. Aroha.
Te wehi. Awha. Ataahua. Na ka whiti te ra.

Di nait aid nof tingz. Luv. Fraidy fraidy. Staam.
Quiatniss. So di sun rise.

The night hides many things. Love. Fear. Storms.
Beauty. The sun rises."

- Am'ayim Saying

The storm had suddenly gotten worse as if Caim himself were throwing his rage at them in the night. Most of the sailors were below decks now, and everything had been battened down. The ship was also anchored, and all they had left to do was to take down the mainsail. For this, someone had to climb up the mast and cut it loose while others waited in the rigging and on deck to catch it. This was to prevent it from being shredded in the wind. To do the task, all Am'ayim crews had a rigging monkey. On the Ariela, this was Rangi.

She held onto the wet center mast with one hand while bracing herself on the foot rope beneath her and took the hatchet she'd been carrying out of her teeth. The wind blew harder and made the foot rope sway beneath her, but she just reorientated herself and rode the movement until it stopped. Then she looked to either side, making sure that Tane, Eyduan, Fadel, and Guafi were all in place to catch the mainsail before swinging her hatchet. She couldn't hear the hatchet strikes, but she could feel them, and it took three to cut through the bolt rope and three again for the rigging. She was strong, but these ropes were made to withstand the Salt. The men caught the mainsail exactly right and started to lower it while rolling the massive thing up. It would take a lot of work to hang it again, but that was better than the storm ripping the thing to shreds. Her father, Captain Bez Masudo, decided not to take the mast down, as this storm didn't look serious enough to break it.

She slowly climbed back down after putting the hatchet back between her teeth. She hated holding it there, but it was safer than the blade swinging in the wind at her belt, and she needed both hands to climb. She hated being the ship's rigging monkey, but they'd chosen her for the post because she was smaller than the men and had better balance, which made sense. A powerful gust of wind shook the rigging near her and she had to hold on for dear life as Caim tried to drag her into the seething river water below.

The wind abated and she started to climb again. This took forever when the ship was wet, and she had to keep stopping for gusts of wind, but she was nearly halfway there. She moved downward again, putting her foot carefully on the next monkey iron, when another more powerful gust of wind hit the ship. Everything swayed and tilted. Rangi's position didn't give her enough support to grab on and she flew into the open air. The wind and lightning seemed to celebrate her fall, flashing and blowing as she plummeted. Thunder echoed the beating of her heart, and at that moment, Rangi knew death was coming for her. There was a moment of regret for herself, not fear, Masudos weren't afraid of death, but to die outside of battle, to such a small, simple thing? Rangi felt regret and shame as the wind tossed her towards the waiting water.

Then, the hard impact of salvation came out of nowhere as the form of another sailor came swinging out of the storm, using the loose mast rigging, and caught her bodily. The breath was knocked out of her, and they hit the deck hard, but she was alive. Rangi pushed herself up on all fours, gasping for breath, and touched fingers to lips, smiling at her luck, before standing up to see who had saved her. Her eyes met the beautiful brown pools of Bayani's and he grinned happily. Of course, it had been him. No one else was foolhardy enough to do what he'd just done for her. Rangi felt something inside of her heart loosen a little and smiled back at him. He was brave, very handsome, and just a little crazy.

"You're all right. I got you, but we should go inside."

Rangi walked up to Bayani, and he looked at her questioningly, but she didn't reply. Instead, while looking into his eyes, she knotted her fist into the waist of his pants and pushed him against the cabin bulkhead before kissing him. The ship moved beneath them with the storm, the wind keened like a living thing, and his arms wrapped around her. Maybe she was more than a little crazy herself.

***

Bez sighed, looking down at the Shatranj board again. He'd been staring out the galley porthole. The storm had gotten worse. He could feel the Ariela rocking back and forth, hear the roaring wind outside, and feel the salty, damp wrath in the air. Thankfully, his crew was skilled and everything had been done in time, even though the mainsail demasting had been a close call, with the wind picking up as they were finishing. He moved his ruhk and looked across the small board at his opponent, Absai.

He'd acquired this board in Royal Seyla's capital of Kinrai, and it was made for ships. Each space had a hole that corresponded to a peg at the bottom of each piece. They still sometimes came out, especially during a bad storm, but it was better than nothing. He would bring it out during storms, bad port delays, or maintenance dockings. Each crew member could challenge him for a shot of Kava, the favorite Am'ayim spirit drink, of which he made sure to always have a small cask aboard.

Absai smiled and moved his elephant. "Fahz."

Bez thumbed his earlobe and looked at the board again. He was getting lost in thought a lot tonight. Maybe it was the storm, the young Weaver, the child with different colored eyes, or maybe he was just getting old. He picked up one of his soldiers, considering his next move carefully. Maybe Tiare would let him retire after this run? Probably not, but he enjoyed thinking about lazy days on the beaches of Ni'Moku. He placed the soldier down, blocking Absai's elephant. "Yuh a get betta."

Absai flashed his gap-toothed smile, already placing his hand onto his ferz. "Tank yuh old fren." He placed down his ferz and Bez smiled. His trap had been sprung.

He moved one of his knights almost without thinking. "Fahz."

Absai looked at the board and laughed. He wasn't a great player, but he could see that the game was over. Bez had caught his shah and ferz in a pincer. "Miebi mi wi biit yu neks taim!"

Bez nodded, wishing he could be above decks, looking at the river and smoking Haze Flower. He hated being cooped up down here all night. He waved his hand. "Yuh can have yuh shot." He looked around at his crew, noticing his daughter and Bayani talking in a quiet corner, then continued speaking. "All a unu can have shots, unu did do gud an tomorrow ago be a day a haad work. Yuh earn yuh kava!" They all cheered and lined up for their drinks, which Bez left for Fatiou to pour because he was tired and went to find his bunk. Bez missed having his cabin.

***

Absai sat on his hammock and swung his legs into it. He'd stayed up much longer than the captain, drinking and talking with the crew. They hadn't gotten too rowdy tonight. There was a storm raging, and they'd have to clean or repair the ship after it broke, but it was nice to have some time and kava with the men.

He sighed tiredly and closed his eyes, thinking about the captain. Bez was getting older. He was more prone to smoking by himself above decks at night, sleeping earlier, and working directly with the crew less. All the prerogative of a captain, but generally telling that Bez Masudo was getting older because he had been quite the rabble-rouser in his day. Absai laughed, remembering the time they'd tried to smuggle a load of gems through port Ni'Moku. Of course, they'd been caught, and oddly, that very event had eventually led Bez to marry Tiare Masudo.

Absai chuckled quietly to himself. From an arrested criminal to a Masudo trade ship captain! Not to mention having one of the most beautiful and deadly women of Ni'Moku as his wife. Bez Masudo was a legend, and Absai had enjoyed being at the man's side through it all. Even now, old and tired, on a regular trade journey, the man has managed to find a young Weaver for a passenger, and now the Ariela was heading to Sceotan. Then that very Weaver had taken in a helpless mother and her child with different colored eyes. Fate and belief were circling around them all. More stories to be remembered!

Absai opened his eyes again and stared at the bulkhead above his cabin. How strong was this Weaver? He'd never seen anyone caught in midair like that. Though, truthfully, he had little to no experience with Weavers, it was just shocking to see the young lady catch him so easily without even trying. Her face had shown no effort like she might have been drinking afternoon tea. He was very curious about what else she could do. For once in his life, he wanted to know about a woman, not because she was a pretty barmaid or a prostitute. She was powerful, smart, and so correct in her mannerisms. He found her intriguing in a way that, previously, he didn't even know existed. But he felt shame for how he had treated her in the beginning.

Absai closed his eyes, sighing tiredly, feeling the effects of the kava, the beating he took from the shorter fall, and working so hard against the storm. He would sleep well tonight, and then it was back to work tomorrow. The life of a sailor never changed much, even when amazing things happened. A sailor lived and died on the Salt no matter what.

***

Rosalie closed her eyes and leaned her forehead against the cabin windows. She was listening to the ship, the Ariela, which sounded very different than usual in the storm. The gentle swaying was gone, and the

81

sailors were relatively quiet this late, but the storm was raging. She could feel the wind beating on the ship as it rocked, hear the creaking groan of wood, and feel the merciless rain beating down upon the deck above. If the Ariela was indeed alive, this must be hell for her.

Rosalie opened her eyes and stood straighter, stretching with one hand on the cabin wall. As she did so, her gaze fell upon her Weaver's ring. Those colorful glimmers that had begun in Haversfjord were a little brighter. There was one very small amber stone on the side. Crilla once told her that amber was the color of vitality, courage, happiness, and good fortune. It was an odd juxtaposition to her thoughts as she looked out into the stormy blackness. The night was late, but she could not sleep. Something was bothering her. What that was still escaped her, but she could sense it somewhere in the raging night. Something was inside of this storm, not weaving, but magic. A thing more ephemeral and older, like a shadow upon the threads that made up the storm. But why here? Was some ancient creature passing nearby, wandering around this cove by happenstance? Or was someone, or something, watching them? She had no way of knowing for sure and that bothered her. Maybe she was just restless and tired.

Rosalie sighed and looked down as the gray and black ship's cat rubbed up against her. She knelt and scratched its ears. "You do not like this weather very much either, do you?" The cat's only response was to purr and rub against her for more attention. Maybe she was just missing her mother and Jonaas. Those sadnesses were still very real.

A little voice came from across the cabin. "Auntie Rosalie, why aren't you asleep?"

She looked over and met Aife's eyes. The young girl was sitting up in their bunk, though Niomh was still sleeping. "I could not sleep, so I decided to watch the storm for a bit. Though I cannot see much outside in the dark night."

Aife smiled and said, "Take the cat with you! This one helps me sleep a lot." She laid back down and hugged the orange ship's cat close before closing her eyes again.

Rosalie chuckled a little to herself. It was a good idea. Aife was a wonderful child. Maybe Aife and Niomh were the reason her ring was showing amber? Rosalie remembered many stormy nights in the barn, talking with her friends and hugging the barn cats while going to sleep. It had been a time of happiness. She only shuddered for a moment and did not cry this time, thinking about hugging Jonaas tonight, thinking about Crilla's loss. Instead, she picked up the gray and black ship's cat and carried it to her bunk. But sleep was still a long time coming as Rosalie stared at the cabin windows from her bunk. She was missing Jonaas, feeling the loss of her mother, wondering what was out there, and feeling the storm's unrest in the ship's rocking movements. She hugged the cat against her face and closed her eyes, crying quietly.

CHAPTER TWELVE: MADALING ARAW (DAYLIGHT)

Early the next morning, Bez knew the storm was over before he opened his eyes because the Ariela's sway had returned to normal. He swung his legs out of the hammock and stood, stretching his old, aching muscles before heading down the passageway. It was barely dawn, but crew members were already moving about, checking for damage, bilging out water from below, and taking ropes or canvas above decks. He stopped at the galley and nodded to Nikau. "Mi woulda like black tea." The man already had a mug ready for him. He'd always been a good galley cook. Bez took it and headed on his way. "Tank yuh."

When he arrived on deck, Absai was already there grumpily watching the crew work from near the hatch. He spat off the railing before speaking, his voice sounding more than annoyed. "Dem a work slowa dan waan uol salt hag pan kava!"

Bez laughed. "Dem a du gud, dem av aad wok fi du an it betta ef wi siel lieta, ina kies eni debris de ina di riva."

Absai glanced at Bez and took his mug, long enough for him to pack his paipa with Haze Flower, then use a striker to light it. The man kept speaking while Bez was doing this. "Yuh waan mi fi reassign Rangi?"

Bez blew a cloud of Haze Flower smoke into the morning air and took a pull of his tea as they started walking the deck. Both of them kept an eye on the crew while they were talking. "No. Shi did waan be aboard as a kruu, suh wi ago treet har dat way."

Absai eyed him for a moment. "Yu a braita man dan mi uol fren. Mi kudn risk mi pikni laif laik dat."

Bez laughed. "Shi a mi daughta, bot shi a waan Masudo tu. Maybe yuh waan try tell Rangi seh she cyan do notn cause it dangerous?"

Absai stopped in the middle of spitting off the bow and choked. "Mi no tink mi waan do dat."

Bez laughed heartily. "Yuh a wise man wen yuh try Absai, tank yuh fi accept har inna di kruu."

Absai nodded. "Shi a waan gud siela an shi wok aad, bot shi kyan bi aad tu."

"Aye, being har fada kyan bi aad tu."

Absai laughed at that. "Mi shuor, beta yu dan mi! Wat bout wi pasinja dem?"

"Dem did deh inna mi cabin all aftanoon an night yeside, mi tink dem ago come out soon. Di young Weaver a waan curious uman an mi sure she ago be ask nuff kweschans soon."

"Yuh waan mi stop har?"

"Mek har so lang shi no tap dem work. Shi did save yuh neck."

Absai looked chagrined. "Aye kyapten, dat a true."

"Mek di kruu set sail afta repairs an stew, wi don lost enough time."

***

Rosalie smiled at Aife, who was still asleep even though morning had come a few hours before. Last night, she spent hours chasing the ship's cats, jumping on their bunk, eating, and helping Rosalie practice her glow orb animals. She woke up late in the night. So Niomh had chosen to let Aife sleep a little longer while they read and discussed the various beliefs of where they were both from. Rosalie was smiling because the thought had occurred to her that being able to sleep in must be a new thing for Aife. She looked so peaceful and happy. It was remarkable how close they had all become in the past weeks, but she supposed it made sense. She and Jonaas had given these two a new chance in life, and they were all in a time when they needed friends and support. She focused on what Niomh had just said, attempting to suppress the thoughts of Crilla and Jonaas that came bubbling to the surface. "Your people really spend an entire two weeks singing and dancing by firelight for the winter solstice?"

Niomh looked up from her reading and smiled. "Yes, we do. The weeks when days get shorter and colder are celebrated with great enthusiasm to bring warmth and love during the winter season. This brings us good luck going into planting season and the new year. We also put trees up inside our homes to celebrate the annual rebirth of life. The entire two-week-long celebration is dedicated to our goddess of the sun, Koliada."

Rosalie closed the book on her lap, looking curious. "Why a sun goddess for that time of year? It is usually so cold, and sometimes it even snows where I am from. Is it different near where your people live?"

Niomh tapped her chin thoughtfully. Every culture was so different, and she needed a moment to think about the right way to explain her people's beliefs. "We are a nomadic people, though much of our time is spent around the vast Tanglewood. We travel almost everywhere, and every land has different seasons. It's more to celebrate what's to come. We look forward to leaving winter's cold, dreary days behind and celebrating the coming of warmth and bounty with spring."

"So the celebration and the request to your goddess are the same thing? That is very interesting. Back home, we would not celebrate the spring until it arrived, though we would make the request for a good season to the goddess before that. The Holy Church of Jhoras, the dominant religion of Acdonia, even had a phrase for requesting the blessing of their deity, paying the tithe."

Niomh arched her eyebrow. "That sounds dreadful. Almost as though your lives would be forfeit without your deities. My people believe faith should be a loving, joyful, and celebrated part of one's life."

Rosalie looked out their small cabin's window. "I think that it comes down to free will."

"What do you mean?"

Rosalie's eyes lost their focus as if she were looking into the distance or thinking about something more important than where she currently was. "Everything in life comes down to free will. Love, happiness, freedom, and even the basic right to exist." She tapped her fingers on the book in her lap, still thinking. "Those who follow The Holy Church have almost no control over their lives. They owe everything to Jhoras and must follow his laws without fail, or they will lose everything. They even have to pay for the right to believe, with taxes and tithes." She looked pointedly at Niomh. "Whereas those who follow one of the goddesses have the ability to live their lives freely, so long as they respect the general values of their people." She smiled thoughtfully. "You can even see the difference in our ways of following the Three Sisters versus your people's goddess Koliada. Your celebration of life and coming joy versus our request for a good season once it has arrived."

"That's the reason you left Jonaas behind, as you mentioned earlier. His ability to live a free life. You are a remarkable young woman."

The thoughts came back. Rosalie felt her face change to sadness, and tears started falling down her cheeks. She looked out the window again and wiped her eyes. "It is, but I miss him so much. I do not know that I am strong enough without him." She looked at Niomh, still crying. "I lost both of them in such a short time. Jonaas and Crilla too."

Niomh got up and went to embrace her. "You are stronger than you think, Rosalie. They both believed in you, and so does everyone who has met you since." Rosalie laid her head down in Niomh's arms and let herself cry.

***

When they finally went above deck, the sky was calm and peaceful. The wind had blown the storm elsewhere during the night. Sailors were running around fixing the few damaged lines and rehanging the mainsail. Niomh smiled, pointing into the distance. "You see, Aife? Soon, we will sail that way on our way home. The Tanglewood is a beautiful forest, and our people are so kind. You will love it."

Her daughter jumped up and down excitedly, clapping her hands. "I'm so excited to see our home, Mama! But what about Auntie Rosalie?"

Niomh smiled, watching her. She'd been afraid the storm would keep Aife up all night, terrified. But between playing with the ship's cats and Rosalie's glow orbs, Aife remained calm and slept deeply. "Rosalie has her own journey ahead of her, remember? She must travel to Sceotan and become a Weaver."

Rosalie hugged her. "Do not worry, we will see one another again. I will never forget you or your mother."

Aife hugged her back tightly. "I won't ever forget you either!"

Rosalie stood back up and, looking at the sky, used a hand to shelter her eyes from the bright morning sun. "It is odd how a large storm can vanish under a stiff wind so quickly. Maybe I need to live near the sea longer to understand."

The captain stopped near them and nodded his usual good morning. "Di Saalt is much diffrent fram lan, staams dem move fast an aad, we did lucky dis waan was short."

Rosalie scanned the ship and all the sailors who were repairing various things after the storm and then looked back at the captain. "How long will repairs take? Was there any serious damage?"

"Di main sail was di worst an dem a rehang it now, wi shuda a sail again soon." With that, he walked away to make sure everything was being repaired properly. He always kept a very watchful eye on his crew.

Niomh watched him go about his duties. "He's not one for long conversations, is he? He has certain other qualities though . . ." She tapped her chin thoughtfully.

Rosalie raised her eyebrows at her. "He is married!"

She laughed. "That he is! But looking doesn't hurt anyone. He's also Am'ayim, and they, more often than not, have more than one wife."

Rosalie's eyes looked about to pop out of her head. "More than one wife!? That is so odd. Things have been so different since I left home."

Niomh laughed while carefully keeping an eye on Aife. "They often have a wife at different ports and even families. It seems odd to those from different places, but to them, this is normal life."

Rosalie watched the captain thoughtfully. "I am most interested in learning about the various cultures around Innatraea." She looked back at Niomh again. "I would like to learn more about your people as well."

Aife jumped in between them. "Mama, I'm hungry. Can we go eat? I hope they have something different than pears, cheese, salted beef, and hard biscuits. I'm so tired of those!"

Rosalie met Niomh's eyes, her look twinkling with laughter. There wasn't much different food available aboard the ship, but her daughter didn't understand that. She was just happy to have food whenever she wanted. That not-so-small thing was still new to them. "We can go see what Nikau has for us soon, sweetling,

"I think he said there would be stew. Let's watch the river for a little while. We're setting sail again soon!"

Chapter Thirteen:
Ngakau'to Asin
(Heart of Salt)

"The Salt is Am'ayim's life. From their birth in the tides to their lives as sailors, everything they are as a people is one with the Salt. Ngakau'to Asin, Heart of Salt, is an honor for those whose very soul represents these beliefs."

- Tavid the Traveler

Later that day, Bayani paused to wipe the sweat off his brow and rest his arms. They were using the docking poles to clear debris away from Ariela as she slowly sailed down the river. It was grueling work, and they'd already broken a few poles, but it was better than a hole in the hull. He sheltered his eyes from the afternoon sun and looked up towards the crow's nest. He should be working, but he couldn't help it. Rangi was up there watching the river ahead of them. They'd started sailing again earlier that day, and it was her job to watch the river ahead for debris. She was so beautiful and strong. He was still shocked at

92

what had happened. He found himself rubbing his fingers along his lips again, remembering what hers had felt like, what her hands on him had felt like and had to shake himself. He had work to do, and standing there staring would likely draw the captain's attention.

Apparently, he had already been seen because Absai stopped near him and regarded him with a look of annoyance. "Yuh shuda a work not a stare like a walrus inna heat."

Bayani looked back down at the river and firmly grasped his docking pole. "Sorry."

Absai looked at him a moment longer before laughing. "Shi priti, bot yu a fuul, shi a waan Masudo an di kyapten daughta tu."

Bayani looked up and met Absai's eyes. "I know that she's a Masudo. That's one of my favorite things about her."

Absai shook his head. "Yu mad laik di kyapten!" He spat off the bow and leaned against the gunwale nearby. He looked more amused now than annoyed. "Yuh andastan weh being a Masudo mean?"

Bayani pushed a small floating log away from the Ariela and then looked at Absai again. "They're a powerful family of strong women. They have always sounded amazing to me, and Rangi has proven that feeling so far."

Absai laughed from his gut, a loud and startling sound from such a big man. "Dat a waan likkle part, some woulda call dem a house a man killers."

Bayani paused for a moment, then started laughing at the absurdity. "People always say strange things about those they don't understand." He looked out across the deck and saw their young Weaver passenger and her two unusual companions, the mother and daughter, all watching the river together. "Take her for example. What have you heard about Weavers before meeting her?"

He couldn't help but think of their strange passengers: a young Weaver, a Danae woman, and her young child with different colored eyes. Hopefully, fate would treat them kindly because he had a feeling that whatever was in store for them was just beginning.

***

Rosalie looked up at the crow's nest as Rangi's voice and a loud clanging bell carried over the Ariela. "Debris inna di riva!" She immediately ran to the front of the ship to see what was happening, instinctively using her power to keep her balance. She did not need Crilla's guidance for this, though her mother's voice always seemed to play in her mind whenever something was happening. She missed her greatly. Crilla was the only mother Rosalie had ever known. *In dire circumstances, actions must be taken swiftly. Weavers do not have the luxury of waiting upon discussion . . .*

She reached the front of the ship with Niomh and Aife right behind her. Captain Masudo, Absai, Fatiou, Bayani, and Masina were already there. "Debris? Is it bad?"

Absai yelled at the top of his lungs. "Drap di anchors!" Then, he started to run off, but Captain Masudo stopped him with a hand on the shoulder.

"It too late, di entire bluff collapse inna a landslide, an di current have wi. Mek di kruu brace fi impact an ready di dinghys."

She looked ahead of them down the river. Enough debris to make an entire cliffside blocked Ariela's path. Dirt, rocks, and trees were strewn across the entire river, creating a massive natural dam. *Always use one's power to help others. There is no higher calling...*

Rosalie stepped forward and started weaving without a second thought for herself. The river swelled around the Ariela, but in the wrong direction, slowing the ship down. The wind picked up, whipping her dress around her, but she ignored it and focused on the massive landslide ahead. She could feel the weight of all the dirt, rocks, and trees. It was far heavier than anything she had ever lifted before. But she had to try. Rosalie focused, weaving everything she had into that giant mound. She could feel her mind straining, like all that weight was being carried by her will, an entire mountain of it. Tears filled her eyes, and she moaned under the strain. Her nose started bleeding, but she did not notice that small thing in the sea of pain that was currently her existence.

She stepped forward again, concentrating. She could feel her body tiring, and her legs faltered, but someone held her up. The debris started to rumble like stones rolling down a hill. It shook, and with it, Rosalie's body shook, too. She sensed cracks now, porous holes, into which water swept. Rosalie could feel that mountain weighing down upon her power and her will, and she pushed back. Tears streamed down her face, and her entire being spasmed, but she held on. Her will was stronger than her body, and these people needed her. She could do this! Crilla's voice spurred her onward. *To use a Weaver's full power is painful and a great risk, but with adversity, we grow...*

Absai spoke nearby, but she didn't see or even hear him. All her focus was on the river and the massive mound of death waiting for them.

Everyone's lives depended upon her now. "Mi neva si so much powa, shi a du it!"

Masina spoke too. "Luk pan ar Weaver ring, it a glow laik aat faiya!"

Other murmurs passed through the crew, as a few of them fell to their knees looking at Rosalie. "Ngakau'to Asin"

Something like a dam, but intangible, broke open inside of her. Rosalie felt her inner being—her will—expand through that new opening and knew she had succeeded. She let go, flowing with that inner tide, as the massive landslide rolled out of their way, rumbling like a great storm of rock and water. The Ariela safely sailed through as the crew cheered, danced, screamed, and stared in disbelief. But Rosalie did not see any of it. She just quietly collapsed into Niomh's arms as the world faded into a blank, featureless darkness.

Aife cried out, terrified. "Mama, is Auntie Rosalie alright? Did she do that? Is she alive?"

***

Serafina watched Rosalie collapse from her place at the shore while their ship drifted through the new gap in the debris left by the avalanche she had caused. The girl was powerful, more so than any Weaver in history. The girl had also chosen to push her will through the doorway and evolve. Very few could even sense that, let alone possess the clarity to make the choice consciously. The girl was impressive.

96

More importantly, she also had a good heart. Not many would have risked themselves so greatly for the sake of others. This spoke well of her, especially since these people were still strangers; she had only met them a few weeks ago. Rosalie and her Vessel's charity towards the lost mother and child was also truly profound. Annoyed as she was to admit it, her sister Rhiannon may have been right about this girl.

Serafina tapped her finger thoughtfully on her chin as she wove invisibility around herself and floated into the sky, still watching. The mother and a few of the crew were carrying Rosalie down into the ship. It was a shame she had left her Vessel behind. Serafina had worked hard to find that young man, but they would meet again; they were tied together by cords stronger than fate. She and her sisters would have to watch Rosalie very carefully. She smiled and shifted back home. They would be meeting soon, and she had much to tell them about this girl who had exercised more power than anyone else on Innatraea only to save a ship full of strangers. That crew was tied to Rosalie now, Ngakau'to Asin was a rare thing, and the Am'ayim always paid their debts.

CHAPTER FOURTEEN: PABAYBAYIN (SHOREBOUND)

"To the Am'ayim, Innatraea's seas, or the Salt, represent both life and death. This struggle is the heart of their people."

- Tavid the Traveler

Manaia felt the sweat pouring down his face, but he couldn't do anything about it. Bez and Fatiou were helping the Danae woman take their young Weaver passenger, Rosalie, down below. She had blacked out after saving the Ariela from destruction, in what he could only describe as the greatest display of power he'd ever seen. But they weren't safe yet. The river had swelled more than it should have from the storm because of the avalanche, and there was still debris everywhere. He looked around the ship at the crew who were acting as spotters. They weren't yelling but instead used hand signals to indicate what was coming, as voices were lost too easily in chaos like this. Responding to a signal from Fadel, he yanked the helm to starboard, holding on tightly as his sweat-slicked hands slipped.

He felt something large and heavy thump against the hull and drag along the ship, followed by the horrible sound of wood creaking and breaking. Hopefully it hadn't hit the Ariela at a bad angle, but there was no way to tell from here. Either someone would come to tell him, or the ship would start taking on water and handling more sluggishly. They needed to get out of this soon. Thankfully, they were almost to where the river flowed into Altin Bozkirlar, or "The Golden Steppes." The vast and relatively flat barren grasslands that eventually surrounded Tursim. There, they should be able to find a shoreline more friendly to landing the ship, where they could rest and make the necessary repairs.

Then, as if Caim himself had been listening to Manaia's thoughts, he saw Huareo lift a closed fist on the Ariela's port side as the alarm bell clanged the port code from the crow's nest above. Which meant there was a large mass of debris ahead on the ship's port side. He took a brief moment to look down the river to starboard and groaned. There were shallow waters ahead; he could tell by how the water was rippling. Usually, the Ariela would never go that close to a river's shore, but the current was flowing fast and judging by the continual alarm sounding their situation was dire. It would be easy to steer too far in this chaos, they should have just waited in the cove.

He hesitated for another moment, but then Bez was back on deck yelling like a man possessed. "Wi a tek aan waata! To starboard! Betta shore bound dan dead!" Manaia spun the helm to starboard as Bez kept yelling commands to the rest of the crew.

Being caught in a situation like this was terrible. Possibly running aground in shallow waters or hitting a large mass of debris was an impossible choice that he was thankful someone else had to make, especially on inland rivers where shores were less stable, rocks more common, and waterways smaller.

Moments seemed to pass with the fast rhythm of his heartbeat as the Ariela sailed through the narrow gap between the shallows and the mass of debris. He could feel the ship sailing slower and handling worse as she took on water, but thankfully, they had just made it into Altin Bozkirlar so they could hopefully find a place to land and repair. Bez came to stand next to him and pointed at a nearby shore. Manaia looked at it and nodded, spinning the wheel again. Bez walked away without a word and started yelling for their ship's carpenter, Sione, as Absai and a few others started readying the anchors and dinghies. They'd made it safely through, but now there was more work ahead. They'd probably have to set up camp for a few days while they careened and repaired the ship. Hard work was part of a sailor's life, though, and they were all alive. He muttered a prayer of thanks to Lux.

***

A few days later, Bez approached his ship's officers' campfire. They had set up around the Ariela on the shore a few days ago, after assessing the extent of damage to the ship. The hull had a sizable hole, but they couldn't repair it until they could careen the Ariela, which they wouldn't do until their young Weaver passenger woke up. She had saved them in an incredible display of power, but she was still asleep, and he refused to do anything further that might cause her harm, which included moving her off the Ariela so they could careen the ship. They had, however, moved the ship to shore in preparation. She was sitting on the shore now with a long makeshift ramp leading to her deck. Bez had never seen anyone like the young Weaver and thanked Lux every morning since that she was with them. The officers were all taking turns looking at a small scrap of canvas Fatiou was passing around. He chuckled to himself, already knowing what this was about. "Unu aal a luk pan di nyuu tatu? Mek mi si it."

Fatiou handed him the small scrap of canvas. The sketch made him smile. The Am'ayim had their ways, and he'd been expecting this since the day their young Weaver passenger saved them all. He shook himself just thinking about what would have happened if she hadn't been there. Every time an Am'ayim almost died, they had won a contest against Caim, their underwater undead god of the sea. Such battles meant new tattoos to remember their victories and celebrate their life. This sketch was for that very purpose. Fatiou was no master artist, but her skills were good enough to inspire a tattooist's piece that one of the Ariela's crew wanted, and they often asked her for sketches when they needed one. This sketch showed a rose with a Weaver's ring around its stem, surrounded by a circle of water and rocks.

He looked around the shore at the stacks of goods and supplies, all surrounded by campfires and his crew. From the older sailors like Ahohako to the calmer ones like Eyduan or Tane, all the way to the rowdy Keahi and other powder monkeys. This time would be different; every crew member's eyes he met showed it, and he expected his eyes did as well. Usually, a tattoo would be for one of them, or in a bad case, for the few who had survived an accident. This time was different. They had all survived thanks to their young Weaver passenger.

Masina interrupted his thoughts as though they could sense what Bez was thinking. "Di young Weaver an di pikni wid diffrent eyes, dem a Lux blessed, mi believe it is fate. Even mi ago get di tatu." This was a bold statement because Masina was their Pirihi, or priest of Caim. It was their job to look after the crew's faith and interpret signs for them. If they were getting the tattoo then the whole crew would without question.

Palani, their night watch master, nodded his bald head along with Masina's words before also speaking. "Mi also believe seh fate a guide wi."

Absai, however, looked concerned. Bez put a hand on the man's shoulder. "Old fren, yuh no believe seh fate guide wi to di young Weaver an pikni?"

Absai rubbed his beard thoughtfully and spat into the fire before replying. "Mi believe seh, mi have anodda problem." He sighed heavily and continued. "Mi a worry bout how mi treat har wen she did first arrive."

Fatiou laughed and slapped Absai on the back. "Yu a tingk tu moch, jos se yu sari."

Neftali, a well-built South Islander and the ship's gunner, was rumbling with laughter. "Yu fried a waan likl gyal pikni!"

Bez just smiled at the joke. He knew what it was like dealing with women of power. "Yuh wi be fine old fren, jus talk to har an seh yuh sorry. Shi stil a waan naamal gyal bihain aal a dat de powa."

Absai nodded, looking a bit chagrined. "Aye, yu rait, mi wi taak tu har. Mi ago get di tatu."

Nikau, the Ariela's galley cook and second-oldest crew member, arrived with a pot of stew and bowls for everyone. Bez noted the younger crew members Salesi, Huareo, and Akua taking pots of stew to the other campfires. "Yuh a talk bout di new tatu? Mi believe all a wi fates dem change dem last few days yah. Di Saalt a shift roun wi like staam breeze, mi ago get di tatu."

Bez smiled, he'd expected as much. He handed the scrap of canvas back to Fatiou. "A gud wok Fatiou, tank yuh, shuo di kruu." He looked at Nikau. "Yuh lef stew fi wi passengers?"

Nikua nodded. "Aye kyapten, it deh by di ship."

He nodded and took one more look around at the campfires where his crew were all getting ready to eat their evening meal before heading towards the Ariela. Bez stopped by the ramp momentarily while picking up the stew bowls Nikau had left. The sight of his ship sitting damaged on the shore was heartbreaking, but at least they were all alive. Bez had been checking on the young Weaver and the child constantly because he was worried. They were both being looked after by Niomh, who said everything was fine. Rosalie was simply resting peacefully because she needed it. He stopped outside the cabin door and knocked, thinking about how odd it still felt to knock on his own cabin door. It opened, and Niomh looked at him. He tried to smile encouragingly. "How everybody deh? Mi bring some stew . . ." He stopped, unsure what else to say as always.

Niomh's expression lightened and she smiled. "She hasn't woken up yet, but she is breathing peacefully. Rest easy, Captain."

He held the stew bowls out to her. "Tek di stew, deh extra in case shi wake up an hungry."

Niomh took the stew bowls from him and smiled softly. "Thank you, Captain." He turned to go but then Niomh's little girl asked something that made Bez freeze in his tracks.

"Mama, you say it like Sharone, right?"

Every Am'ayim knew that name; the Weaver who held it was a legendary hero among their people. He turned back towards the door and gently put his hand on it to stop Niomh from closing it. She looked at him curiously. "Peace, mi mean no disrespect. Yuh a talk bout Weaver history? How yuh pikni know dat deh name?"

Niomh smiled. "We were talking about Rosalie. Aife wanted to make sure she could pronounce it the right way. It is Rosalie's family name."

Bez's heart skipped a beat and his mouth worked silently for a few moments before he could speak. "Lux above, fate have mercy pan dis kruu!"

Niomh's eyes seemed to take on a more focused look. "What do you mean, Captain?"

"Di Weaver weh bear dat deh name, shi a waan hero mongst Am'ayim. Weh Rosalie mada niem?"

Niomh leaned against the door frame and sighed. "Crilla Sharone, I am sure it's her." Bez's heart skipped another beat, and he had to remind himself to breathe again. Fate had a hold of him and his crew. Niomh looked out across the ship into the darkening evening before looking back at Bez. "My people have a saying. I was thinking of it just a few days ago during this voyage. Seme ando Balval. It means Seeds in the Wind." She sighed tiredly, closing her eyes. "My people believe that sometimes the winds of fate must move an Innatraean to where they belong." She opened her eyes and glanced into the cabin, most likely looking at Rosalie. "We may all be caught in the web of her destiny." She looked back at him and said, "Sleep well, Captain. I believe we all need the rest." With that, she finally returned to the cabin while balancing the stew bowls carefully and shouldered the door closed.

Bez walked back towards his officers on shaky legs. He nodded to the crew at every campfire on his way and shook his head. They were all concerned and wanted to know if their young Weaver passenger had woken yet. He had shared their concern when he thought their young Weaver was just a random girl who happened to be capable of doing what was impossible. Now, he knew she would be fine because she was the daughter of Crilla Sharone. One of the most legendary heroes known amongst his people who wasn't Am'ayim. None of it was a coincidence. He could see it all, from his courting Tiare to joining House Masudo and his daughter Rangi fighting to be allowed aboard the Ariela to the young Bayani proving himself worthy on the streets of Kinrai. Everything had led them all to this. Fate had them like a vice, and it culminated in something his old friend Absai had said at the very beginning when the young Weaver had requested ka'u malihini kaumatau. *How shi know bout dat? Mi no tink shi a gud idea kyapten.* Thinking about how prophetic that moment had been made Bez laugh as he arrived at the officer's campfire. They looked at him curiously. "Gather di kruu, mi have someting fi tell everybody."

Chapter Fifteen: Dagat ng Panahon (Sea of Time)

> *"O galu o le taunuuga e pei o Le Sami, malosi ma le le mautonu.*
>
> *Di waves a destiny dem a like Di Saalt, powerful an unpredictable.*
>
> *The waves of destiny are like the Salt, powerful and unpredictable."*
>
> *- Am'ayim Saying*

Rangi looked up from the crates she was lounging on when she heard Absai's sharp whistle. He was the Ariela's Bosun and knew how to get their attention, but it still took a few minutes for everyone around the camp to quiet down and look. They were sailors, free women and men, and only paid attention out of respect or necessity. Her father was there, too, and she could see the other officers behind the two men. Whatever they had to say must be important. Maybe it was about the young Weaver. Had she finally woken up?

Her father, Captain Bez Masudo, stepped forward and began speaking. "Mi a nuh man a eligant words, but mi have someting very important fi tell uni all." This made Rangi smile to herself. Was her father not a man of words? He knew the language of every port they sailed to and always spoke with such intelligence. She was so proud of him. He cleared his throat and continued. "Unu all know di stories bout Crilla Sharone?" He paused for a moment and looked around the camp as if judging the nods of each crew member as an answer to his question. Everyone knew exactly who that specific Weaver was. She was a legendary hero among their people. What did she have to do with the crew and her father?

Bez crossed his hands behind his back. Absai shifted nervously on his feet and the wind seemed to pick up momentarily as her father spoke, causing the fires around their camp to stir. Rangi leaned forward to catch her father's words better. There was something different in the air, she could feel it. "Wi young Weaver pasinja, Rosalie. Har family name is Sharone, she a Crilla's daughta." Rangi gasped. Dagat ng Panahon had them all in its currents, fate was in charge of all their destinies now; may Lux have mercy upon their souls.

As if to echo her thoughts, a murmur ran through the entire camp as sailors everywhere stirred. Absai opened his mouth to speak and Masina stepped up next to Bez. But her father raised his hand and looked around the camp, meeting each sailor's eyes until they quieted. "Sins shi siev aal a wi laif wi each been a kweschan wi fates, an a talk to Masina." Her father lowered his hand now that they were listening. "Each a unu have unu own stories, unu reasons fi deh yah, an unu own beliefs inna fate. But wi all deh yah now an mi believe Dagat ng Panahon have wi inna it powa." He crossed his arms behind his back again and took on a more serious tone, both in voice and expression. "Each a unu have a choice fi mek wen we reach Tursim. Yuh can stay aboard Di Ariela an see weh fate have fi wi, or set yuh sails loose an see weh di wind tek yuh." He closed his eyes but then looked up and continued. "Legends a one exciting ting, an mi believe fate ago lead wi deh, but fate isn't gentle an wi a head fi di haad Saalt." Her father's eyes seemed to glow with the light of the nearby campfire. "Know dis. Mi fully dedicated to dis path."

After that, her father quieted and awkwardly motioned for Masina to speak, which amused Rangi. It wasn't often that something caught her father off guard or gave him pause, but the fates of their entire crew were in the balance, so she understood. Rangi focused on Masina as they started speaking. Their words here would count for even more than the captain's since they were the ship's Pirihi, making it their job to interpret signs.

Masina kept their words short. They weren't one for long speeches or explanations, but every sailor was quiet and listening in rapt attention. "Mi agree wid di kyapten. Wi young Weaver a di daughta a waan legendary hero, an she hab a pikni companion wid diffrent eyes. Di sign dem clear, a fi wi fate." They paused and looked out into the night. "Dagat ng Panahon have wi all unda it powa."

As Masina quieted and stepped back, it was clear that Absai also wished to speak, which made sense because he was the ship's Bosun, and the crew was his business. He stepped forward and crossed his arms, silently taking a moment to think with his eyes closed. This was his way before any serious conversation; they all knew it well. When he opened his eyes and started speaking, Absai also looked around their camp, meeting the gazes of every crew member. "Mi owe all a unu a debt, wen di young Weaver first arrive mi neva treat har wid respect, an mi feel bad bout dat." He looked into the flames of the nearby campfire. "Mi ago be seh sorry fi dat, an mi stan wid di kyapten fi dis, a mi fate."

Normally, in important discussions after the officers were done talking, the crew would start joining in the conversation. Am'ayim were not a subtle people and had no issue sharing their opinions. But fate and faith were things of a more personal nature. Each sailor would want their chance to discuss it amongst their friends, any officers they were close to and their ship's Pirihi Masina. So after Absai was done, the officers started dispersing amongst the campfires to join in conversations wherever they were invited. Rangi, however, stayed where she was, quietly thinking to herself. She could see the moments leading her into fate's clutches. From her aunt being unable to bear children to Rangi herself being born and named as their next Reyna, The Flower of Ni'Moku, and even fighting her mother for her right to serve aboard the Ariela. She had fought so hard for her freedom as a strong woman and now fate seemed to be having its way with her after all. What was she going to become? What were they all going to become?

Rangi looked around the camp at their crew, almost all engaged in conversation about exactly what she was thinking, but they were excited and looking forward to being legends. She caught sight of Bayani and couldn't hope but smile as she remembered the night of the storm. Her mother. Her father. The Ariela. This young Weaver, Rosalie. The child with strange, different-colored eyes. Fate. They all seemed to want something of her. Rangi smiled as she stood and made eye contact with Bayani. He smiled, too, and she nodded toward the nearby trees before walking out into the dark night. He would follow her. Tonight, she would take something for herself.

***

Bayani carefully walked out into the night and headed towards the trees, leaving the camp's flickering firelight. He had seen Rangi walk this way after looking at him, and that look had said, *"Follow me, I want you."* She was such a strong woman, deadly, beautiful, and completely sure of herself, yet her heart was hidden behind all that bravado. She had swayed into the night, gracefully flowing away from the light like this world belonged to her, and she expected it to follow her will. Bayani laughed a little to himself at that, because it was exactly what he was doing. He saw a feminine shadow standing under a tree ahead and went to it. "Rangi?"

She turned around and looked at him. He could see her face now that they were closer together. She reached out her hand and touched his cheek. Were those tears on her face? He must be seeing things. Nothing made Rangi cry. She stepped onto a nearby rock and looked down into his eyes, running her fingers through his hair. "Mi did a memba di stuori bout ou mi mada an mi fada fos miit." She leaned into him as if to kiss him, but instead, her face slid past his as she bit his ear gently before whispering softly to him. "Most Masudo umen, wen dem feel dis way, dem ago hit yuh. Mi naa go eva hurt yuh Bayani, but yuh a fi mi."

He smiled. "You didn't seem to mind hitting me in our fight a few days ago."

Rangi smiled, running hand along the side of his face. "Di ring different, mi bwoy. Weh it deh inna wi haat mi naa go eva hurt yuh."

Bayani swallowed before speaking, his mouth suddenly feeling dry. "I thought you said the storm was a one-time thing? That we couldn't because I am a shore child?"

110

Rangi stepped down from the rock and laid her head against his chest. Bayani felt his heart quicken as he realized she was crying. Not knowing what else to do, he wrapped his arms around her. She choked up again before speaking, obviously overcome with emotion. "Yu neva seh dat agen, wi a sail Dagat ng Panahon, an no nuo we a kom fi wi. Mi ago have waan ting fi miself, yuh."

"Your family . . ." She put a finger on his lips to silence him. Then, she looked into his eyes.

"Yu pramis mi nou mi bwoy, no kier bout we ada piipl tink, yuh a fi mi."

Bayani hugged her tighter. "I promise I am yours, and the opinions of others don't matter."

Her hands went to his waist and untied his trousers as she stepped back far enough to pull them down. One of her hands went between his legs as she stepped closer again. "Gud bwoy."

Bayani ran his hands down Rangi's sides and rested them on her hips as she pressed her bare chest against him. He sighed as her hand went to work between his legs and she bit his neck gently. Thoughts of fate, destiny, and what Dagat ng Panahon had in store for them faded, and there was only Rangi.

Chapter Sixteen: Manawa (Breathe)

"Okioki toa, mo apopo te tupuhi.

Rest hero, fi tomorrow di staam a come.

Rest hero, for tomorrow the storm comes.

- Am'ayim Saying

After her conversation with Captain Masudo, Niomh shut the door, set the bowls of stew on the cabin's small table, and sat in one of the chairs. She looked over at Rosalie, who was still asleep in her bunk. The young woman appeared to be resting peacefully, but she hadn't moved aside from the occasional gentle stirring since saving them all from the landslide, and that had been a few days ago. When would she wake up? Was she all right? Niomh had been doing what she could to get water and stew or gruel into Rosalie, but it wasn't much. She sighed and looked over at her daughter, who was happily feeding small pieces of leftover cheese to the ship's cats. Her daughter's eyes seemed to glow in the cabin's dim lantern light.

Niomh's mind drifted back over their journey and the recent conversation with Captain Masudo. Seme ando balval. Her daughter's different colored eyes, Rosalie's young friend Jonaas saving them, and, of course, their voyage with Rosalie herself. What did fate have planned for them? Niomh smiled softly to herself. She was worried about her daughter and Rosalie, but part of her knew they would be all right because fate wasn't done with them yet. "Aife? Come eat, please. The captain brought some stew. After you're done, you can help me try to feed Rosalie."

Aife jumped up and bounded over to the small table, much to the ship cats' dislike. "Mama, can I eat next to Auntie Rosalie? Do you think she will wake up soon?"

Niomh smiled. Her daughter had become very attached to Rosalie over their voyage, but it was well because she was a very kind-hearted young woman, and Niomh felt their fates were more intertwined than even the Am'ayim believed. "I'm sure Rosalie will be fine. She's a very strong young woman and a Weaver. She just needs time. You can eat by her, sweetling. But try not to make a mess and make sure the ship's cats don't steal your stew like last time."

"I promise, Mama, I'll be careful!"

Niomh had to laugh softly to herself because her daughter's promise only lasted a few seconds. Stew sloshed out of her bowl while she was walking to sit by Rosalie again. Niomh sighed and leaned back in her chair. She didn't have the energy to clean it right now, and besides, the ship's cats would get to the food in short order. She looked out the cabin's windows at the dark evening, lost in thought again. There was so much happening, and their fates were still unknown, but she and, more importantly, her daughter were both safe. Niomh closed her eyes to rest for a few moments.

After a short while, her daughter Aife's voice woke her. "Mama, Auntie Rosalie is waking up!"

Niomh carefully went to sit by them both on the bunk. "Sweetling, please put your stew on the table so it doesn't spill." Aife did as she was told while Niomh looked at Rosalie, who stirred again in her sleep. Her eyes moved back and forth before slowly fluttering open. She smiled warmly and, out of habit like she would for her daughter, put her hand on the young woman's head and gently stroked her hair. "You're awake. How do you feel?"

Rosalie tried to sit up, but her face scrunched up in pain and she laid back down. "Like I have been run over by a wild horse." She closed her eyes for a moment and sighed, then opened them again and looked at Niomh. "Did the Ariela and everyone make it through the landslide all right?"

Niomh smiled and comfortingly touched Rosalie's face with her hand. "Yes, everyone is safe because of you. There was some trouble afterward, though."

Just then, her daughter came back and excitedly sat down on the bunk again. "Are you all right, Auntie Rosalie? You're so strong! I want to be like you when I'm older!"

Rosalie smiled softly and slowly put one of her hands on Aife's. She was obviously still tired and weak. "Thank you, little one, that means so much to me." She looked at Niomh. "What trouble?"

"There was a lot of debris in the river after you cleared the landslide, and the Ariela's hull was breached. The crew has been waiting for you to wake so they can careen and repair the ship."

Rosalie tried to sit up again, but a look of frustration crossed her face as she lay back down and winced in pain. She met Niomh's eyes again before closing them, and tears started dripping down her cheeks. "I am sorry. I did not mean for that to happen to the ship."

Niomh stroked Rosalie's hair gently again. "You have nothing to apologize for. What you did saved all of our lives." Rosalie opened her eyes again and they looked at each other. "You must be very hungry. I will help you eat some stew before you rest again. Aife, would you please go and get the other stew bowl?" Her daughter happily went to go do as told while Niomh helped Rosalie sit up. "You need to eat some real food now that you're awake. I did what I could, but you have been asleep for a few days."

After Aife carefully handed the stew bowl to her mother, Rosalie patted a spot next to herself. "Come sit by me, little one. I do not think I will be able to eat all this stew myself, and you can tell me about what I missed."

Aife sat next to her and started talking immediately. "I'm so glad you're awake, Auntie Rosalie! Everyone was worried. My mama and I were just here with the cats and the captain came to check on you so many times!"

As they ate, Aife continued to regale Rosalie with tales of the ship's cats, the captain checking her, and how boring being stuck inside was. When they were finally done, Niomh had Aife put the empty stew bowl aside and helped Rosalie lay back down. "Sleep now. You still need the rest." Surprisingly what she said worked because Rosalie laid her head on the pillow and was sleeping again a few moments later.

Aife came to sit by them, looking concerned. "Mama, do you think Rosalie, Bez, the ship, and everyone will be all right?"

Niomh carefully got up and went to sit on their bunk before patting the spot next to her. When her daughter sat down, she spoke. "I'm sure everyone will be fine, sweetling. It's been a hard journey, but everyone here is strong, and so is the ship. Try not to worry."

Aife was quiet for a moment as if considering her words. "Mama? We have been through so much. Please don't keep things from me."

Niomh hugged her daughter close as tears came to her eyes, remembering all their hardships. "Lay down sweetling, it's time for us to sleep too."

***

A few evenings later, Rosalie slowly walked onto the Ariela's deck. It was late at night, but Innatraea's moons, named after the Three Sisters, were shining brightly. Niomh and Aife were sleeping, but she desperately needed the fresh, cooler night air. Days of weakness, crying over her mother, aching for Jonaas, and being stuck in the ship's cabin had taken their toll. She stopped at the ship's railing and placed her hands there, sighing. Oddly, there was a small carving in the railing where she placed one of her hands. She traced it idly with her fingers. It was a small star, just like the one on the cover of Jonaas' favorite book, Tavid the Traveler, which made her smile. Rosalie missed him so much. She could still imagine his touch, his smell, how it felt when he held her. She missed

Crilla. She even missed Edmond. Trying to avoid her tears, she looked at her ring. It had changed again after the river. The small amber stone was larger now and had a fiery red color at its center. It made her think of the happiness and passion she had shared with Jonaas. Sighing sadly, she gazed out over the large Am'ayim campsite, which was made up of campfires surrounded by stacked supply crates and sailing equipment she could not name. Many of the fires were already out, though a few were still lit, either for the night watch or the few sailors having quiet late-night conversations. Rosalie closed her eyes, enjoying the cool night air as a soft breeze blew over her. Then she heard footsteps behind her. A dark form emerged from the night. She was not worried; women were completely safe amongst the Am'ayim; Niomh had even told her the captain had checked on her so often that it was a nuisance.

The sailor was young and well-muscled like everyone else. He had short brown hair and light brown eyes. They had not talked previously, but Rosalie knew his name was Bayani from days of observation, listening to them all talk, and the fight with Rangi early on, especially since he spoke differently than anyone else on their crew. He smiled and nodded, then touched two of his fingers to his lips briefly before talking. "Good evening, Weaver."

Rosalie smiled. "Please call me Rosalie. Your name is Bayani, correct? What did that gesture of touching your lips mean?"

Bayani smiled, obviously amused and joined her at the railing. The crew always seemed amused by her questions about their ways, but they were polite and answered her every time. "Yes, I am Bayani. The gesture is called Whakaute. It is a silent gesture that means respect. This is a phrase often used for someone of higher rank aboard our ships or for someone whom we greatly admire and owe for something."

"I see. So it is paying respect to me for what I did on the river. I understand, thank you."

"Yes, that is right."

"I noticed that you speak differently than the other crew members. Why is that?"

Bayani crossed his arms and leaned against the railing. He seemed to be considering whether to answer her question. "I didn't grow up on the islands like them; I was born in Kinrai."

Rosalie couldn't help but smile, thinking about Jonaas. "Kinrai, really? How interesting! One of my friends is going there because of his love for Shatranj. We used to read about it when we were children. Is it a nice city?"

"Kinrai? It's a nice enough place for travelers, especially those there for Shatranj or the Aisna. Even if he's not that skilled a player, he should enjoy his time there." Bayani stood and headed towards the makeshift ramp that led off the ship. "If you will excuse me, Weaver, I have my patrol to finish."

"Bayani? Call me Rosalie, please. Ser Kehlmar said Jonaas was an excellent player. He even beat the man twice while we were in Haversfjord. So I am sure he will find Kinrai welcoming. Thank you."

Bayani paused for a moment before heading down the ramp, looking more than a little surprised. "He beat Magnus Kehlmar?! Yes, I am sure your friend will be at home there then. Kehlmar is a very well-known champion. You and your friend are quite interesting people." He hesitated. "Can I ask you a question?"

She smiled. "Of course, what is it?"

He pointed at her hand. "Your ring looks different now. We all saw it glow when you saved everyone on the river. Is it magic, too?"

It was good to talk about things she knew, conversation helped. "Weaver's rings are indeed magic. They represent a Weaver's inner being and change throughout the wearer's lifetime as they too change."

He looked thoughtful. "That is very interesting. The gem colors represent meaning?"

She nodded. "Yes, that is true in most cases. Amber and red usually mean courage and passion."

"Those colors are also important among our people and have similar meanings. Thank you for speaking with me so openly. You are truly kind. Have a good evening, Rosalie."

"You as well, Bayani. Talking helped, thank you." After he left, Rosalie leaned against the ship's railing again and closed her eyes. Talking about her ring brought back memories of Jonaas—their love, their times in bed together, and then home, and her mother. Tears started coming again before she knew it. All of it hurt so much when she really thought about what she had lost and left behind.

Then Aife's small voice interrupted her descent into sorrow. "Auntie Rosalie, you couldn't sleep? Why are you crying?"

She tried to smile and turned around as Aife came to hug her. "I am all right, little one. I am just a bit sad. I was remembering some things about my home."

"You mean about the boy you loved and your mother?"

Rosalie could not help laughing softly as she hugged Aife in return. "You heard us talking about them? You were supposed to be asleep."

"I know, but you and my mama only talk about the good things when I'm asleep." She rested her head against Rosalie. "I'm sorry you feel sad, but you can talk to me too. My mama tries to protect me, but I remember where we came from."

Rosalie mussed up Aife's hair with her hand. "I am feeling much better, thanks to you and your mother. You both did a wonderful job looking after me." Then she took Aife's small hand in her own. "Come along, little one. We should both get back to bed. It is very late."

"Auntie Rosalie, can I sleep by you?"

"Of course you can. Maybe that will help us both get some rest."

Chapter Seventeen: Power and Expectations

"A Weaver's power creates faith in those around them like a fire creates warmth. Act wisely, for their hearts have now become your concern."

- Amah: The Morals of the Weave

A few days later, Rosalie tried to ignore the cold morning wind as it blew through her hair, making a mess of it, even though Niomh had gone through the trouble of brushing it for her earlier. She had been feeling stronger each day and had wanted to do this much sooner, emerging from hiding in the ship's cabin to find out the specifics of their situation. Until this morning, Niomh's objections about her need to rest had won over her urgent curiosity. Now, she was regretting that as a new weakness assaulted her. She was standing on the gravelly shore, where the makeshift ramp ended and the crew's large camp began. Every single one of them was standing still, looking at her, and touching their fingers to lips. The cold wind blew her hair again as Bayani's words came to her mind. *The gesture is called Whakaute. It is a silent gesture that means respect.*

The cold wind blew her hair again, and she tucked it behind her ear distractedly as another thought came to her, one from her favorite book, written by an ancient Weaver named Sister Amah that detailed the morality of their power. *Act wisely, for their hearts have now become your concern.* What was she supposed to do? What was she supposed to say? She was not even halfway through her journey to Sceotan yet. She was still a child where being a Weaver was concerned. Rosalie closed her eyes and took a deep breath. This was the responsibility of her power, and her mother had prepared her for this. She was strong enough for this; she had to be.

Captain Masudo came to stand beside her and put a hand on Rosalie's shoulder. "Powa is a haad ting at yuh age, dem woulda undastan if yuh nuh have no words fi speak."

Rosalie opened her eyes, banishing the vision of her mother and the pang of sadness she felt inside. The captain's hand somehow helped her stand a little taller and feel more up to the task at hand. "Thank you, Captain Masudo, but my power bears responsibility, too. I must speak to them. It is my duty now."

If he had been her father, she would have said he looked proud. "Aye, dat a di right ting fi do." He looked as though there was more to say but stepped back, remaining quiet for now. She would have to ask him later.

Having finally decided what to say, Rosalie looked at the crew and squared her shoulders. A few weaves of air made her voice loud enough for them all to hear. Before speaking, she touched her index and middle fingers to her lips for a moment, seeing many of the crew nod approvingly, confirming it had been the right thing to do. "Respect is a strange thing that nearly every person on Innatraea views differently." She looked at Bayani. "Thank you, Bayani, for teaching me the meaning of this among your people, and to Captain Masudo for watching over me so carefully." She could practically feel him smiling behind her and could see the look of pride on Bayani's face. She looked down for a moment before continuing. "In truth, I also owe each of you a debt. You brought me farther on my journey than I could have gone on my own, and more importantly, you all kept me safe while I slept after overusing my power." She looked around their camp at all their faces, beaming with pride and joy. "For that, I will never forget you so long as I live." Rosalie felt her cheeks color as she finished speaking and their camp erupted in cheers.

Captain Masudo spoke quietly from behind her. "Lux above, dis a di girl whose words mi did a worry bout?"

Before she could reply, Aife came barreling into her and took her hand. "Can we go walk into the camp now, Auntie Rosalie?"

She looked up to make sure Niomh was also there before answering. "We have to look at the damage to the ship first, little one." As they started walking, she noticed the captain take his pipe out. After looking in her direction, the man fumbled it back into his pocket. "Captain Masudo?"

He looked at her, obviously a bit startled, as if he had been thinking about something else. He was an experienced man, though and gathered himself quickly. She still made a mental note to speak with him more later. "Yea, Weaver?"

"You are old enough to be my father. The Ariela is your ship, and I know nothing about sailing. You may smoke your pipe if you wish, you are in charge here, I am merely your passenger."

He looked amused, chagrined, and thankful all at the same time, if that was possible. Though he did take his pipe out again before replying. "Tank yuh Weave, a man's paipa a waan important ting."

She smiled in return. "Address me as Rosalie, please. Now, would you mind leading the way? I am eager to know more about our current situation." He nodded but did not reply as he was busy happily lighting his pipe. She squeezed Aife's hand gently. "Little one? Would you like to walk ahead with Captain Masudo? I need to have a word with your mother."

Niomh came up beside her as Aife ran ahead to join the captain. "I think my daughter loves you as much as any of the crew."

Rosalie nodded solemnly. "I wanted to apologize. Aife has been sleeping at my side, calling me family, and giving me more authority than I should have. You are her mother and this was not my intention."

Niomh laughed with great amusement. "Among my people, children are raised by all of their family and friends. You have nothing to apologize for. If my daughter grows up to have even half of the heart that you do, I will call it more than a fair bargain."

***

For that, I will never forget you so long as I live.

Absai was leaning against a palm tree in their camp as the young Weaver, Rosalie, finished her speech. Everyone in the camp was cheering or clapping, slapping each other on the backs, or showing her Whakaute. He was ashamed of how he'd treated her when she first arrived on the Ariela and had no idea how to apologize while not looking like a fool. But he owed her a debt now, they all did, and he had to make amends. He watched as the small party made their way to the Ariela's hull where Sione, the ship's carpenter, awaited. Sighing, Absai spat onto the ground then pushed himself up and went to join them.

As he approached the small group, Rosalie glanced his way long enough to note his presence, then put her hand near the damaged section of the hull and looked at Sione. "Thank you for explaining the repair process to me. How long will it delay us? Are the repairs very difficult?"

Sione rubbed his short beard, obviously in thought, before replying. "All repairs pan shore haad, but mi only expect dem fi tek a few days."

Bez nodded, thumbing his earlobe momentarily and smoking his paipa. "Aye, dat soun right. Sione staat di wok." He looked at Absai. "Tell di kruu." Then he looked at Rosalie, a bit nervous, which he couldn't blame his friend for at all. She was a powerful woman. "Mi sari fi di delay tek lang Weaver." There was a momentary pause as if Bez was reminding himself of something. "Rosalie, mi hope it nuh a truble?"

She smiled graciously before replying and Absai had to shake himself. There was power and respect in everything she did. Eventually, this young Weaver would rival kingdoms. "You have nothing to worry about, Captain Masudo. Though I am eager to reach Sceotan and start my new life, there is no actual need to hurry in my journey. A few extra days of rest may indeed benefit me." For some reason, she and the Danae woman looked at one another before smiling at the last comment.

Bez looked relieved. "Tank yuh, Rosalie." There was another pause when he spoke her name as if it was taking him some getting used to it. "Wi ago try fi get di wok dun faas."

Rosalie nodded and smiled. "I would prefer that your crew work safely rather than rush. If you do not mind, I will borrow Absai for a few moments before he does as you ordered?"

He felt his mouth drop open and work soundlessly for a moment as his old friend walked away smiling. "Tek yuh time, mi can tell di kruu miself."

Rosalie nodded. "Thank you." She looked at the Danae woman, Niomh, and her daughter. "Niomh? I will join you shortly. Please find a place near one of the campfires for us."

Niomh nodded, taking her daughter's hand after a curious look between Rosalie and herself, and then followed Bez into the camp. "Of course. Come along, sweetling. Rosalie will join us soon."

Rosalie started walking down the shore at a leisurely pace. "Please come join me, Absai." He joined her hesitantly, unsure of what to say and trying to organize his thoughts. She stopped and looked out across the river as a breeze seemed to appear out of nowhere. Her seemingly casual use of magic power made him nervous, even if it did help with the heat. "Absai?" He looked at her. "Please stop looking like a surprised ship's cat and tell me what you wanted to speak with me about." His eyes must have widened. "You have been looking as though you wanted to speak with me since I came into the camp."

How did she know everything so easily? It was true, though. Absai had been thinking about this long and hard, which was new to him. Even respectful sailors treated women who weren't Am'ayim a certain way, but she was different. Sometimes, when faced with impossible tides, you had to just sail the course. He took a deep breath and let it out, then resisted the urge to spit into the water before speaking. "Mi did waan se mi sari fi ou mi chriit yu wen yu riich. Mi neva andastan uu unu bi an mi fiil shiem."

She smiled gently while still looking out over the river. "I see." She spoke again after a moment's pause. "Absai?" He nodded to indicate he was paying attention. "Have you seen how I treat every crew member, even those of low rank such as Akua, with the utmost respect?"

He had indeed seen that now that he thought about her actions that way. "Aye, mi si dat, it gud."

"That is the secret Absai. The respect you give others is not about who they are, or what they have done for you." She turned and met his eyes in a very focused, almost disconcerting way. "It is about who you are inside, and what kind of person you want to be." She looked back towards the camp. "Every Innatraean deserves respect and the freedom to be themselves. Thank you very much for reminding me of that Absai." She met his eyes again, but her look was gentler this time. "I think you would benefit from thinking about this for a little while."

She turned to go back towards the camp, but he had to ask her a question. "Ow yuh know everyting so well, wen yuh til a pikni?"

She turned back. "Pikni is your people's word for a child, correct?" He nodded. She laughed awkwardly and then smiled sadly. "I was just thinking about this earlier. My mother taught me that being a Weaver also means being what others need. It is the responsibility of our power."

As she left, Absai found himself staring out across the river lost in thought. About what she had said, how his old friend treated others, and how he felt when the crew gave him respect. He closed his eyes. Dagat ng Panahon had them all, and just like her he had a responsibility. To the crew, his old friend Bez, Rosalie, and to himself. It was time for him to change. In that moment of clarity and silence—a new thing to him—Absai made a promise to be a better man.

Chapter Eighteen:
O Drom e Phirutnesko
(The Way of Movement)

"Many Innatraeans have lost fortunes to witness Ilo Thaj Jag, the Danae dance of heart and fire."
- Tavid the Traveler

Niomh looked around the large campsite from her place by the officers' fire. The entire crew was eating, talking, drinking, playing music, or even dancing. The scene reminded her of Koliada back home. She shook off the sad memories of her last festival before she'd left her people. They'd worked hard today and deserved the night of revelry. Careening the ship, scraping the hull, and helping Sione with repairs was not an easy task. Then Aife tugged on her sleeve insistently. "Mama, Akua asked me to dance with him! Can I go? It looks like so much fun!"

Her first instinct was to say no. Keeping her daughter nearby meant safety and protection. But then she saw how excited Aife was and thought back over their journey. She'd been on ships where the crew would have forced their way into the cabin and taken them, especially when Rosalie was incapacitated. But these sailors were Am'ayim; they'd proven themselves kind, and she'd seen how they respected Rosalie now after what had happened on the river. She and her daughter were safe here. "Yes, sweetling, go ahead, but don't go too far."

Her daughter was already running off into the camp excitedly as she replied. "I'll stay close, Mama, I promise!"

Rosalie looked over at her and smiled. "It is good to see Aife becoming more like a normal little girl."

Niomh couldn't help but smile back. Their life had been hard, but now there was happiness, too. "Yes, she is happy. You had a lot to do with that. Thank you."

Rosalie nodded awkwardly, as she often did when receiving compliments. It was a reminder of how young she was and how isolated her hometown had kept her. "My pleasure, traveling with you both and the Am'ayim has been an honor. Each of you has taught me more about the Weaver I want to be and how I wish to move through and influence Innatraea during my life."

Niomh smiled warmly and nodded. "Very interesting choice of words. My people's lives are based upon movement." Everyone was enjoying the evening. They were dancing, singing, eating, and drinking. She smiled at the sight of her daughter dancing with Akua at one of the other campfires. "I already told you about my journey of sorrow." She held back the tears this time. "There is another belief we hold called Seme ando Baval, or Seeds in the Wind. It means that sometimes fate moves you, even through hardship, so that you're in the right place."

Rosalie met her eyes. "I am sorry you and Aife had to go through that. I can only hope things get better from here. I am not sure that I believe my destiny has pulled you both like that, however. I am still just beginning my journey, but you may be right." A look of something distant and troubling crossed her face as she fell silent looking over the camp.

Oddly, the ship's officers, including Captain Masudo, who were all sitting at their same campfire, were silently staring at them, paying rapt attention. Niomh smiled, it was time to lighten the mood. This night was for celebration. "All these things fall under O Drom e Phirutnesko, the Way of Movement, but they are the spiritual sides of it. There are things of a more physical nature as well. I used to be a dancer and tonight is a good time for it. I will show you." She stood, leaving her cloak behind, and almost laughed at just how focused their audience's eyes suddenly became; the Am'ayim, it seemed, knew about Danae dancing. Fatiou seemed especially interested, so Niomh touched her gently as she swayed past, earning a very appreciative smile.

As she found a good place by the fire, Niomh noticed that most of the camp had realized what she was doing. The loud chatter came to a stop. Even the usually wild powder monkeys were quietly watching her now, especially Kai and Fetu, who both got an amused slap on the shoulder from Iraia, their small group's only woman. Niomh started to sway gently as the two ship's musicians. Both South Islanders, Baako and Jimani, took up the cadenced beat of Ilo Thaj Jag. She was surprised they knew it, but Am'ayim did travel far. Though their beat wasn't exactly correct it was close enough. Niomh started to flow into the dance, her body remembering happier times.

Rosalie was watching Niomh dance. It was one of the most amazing things she had ever seen. The woman seemed to transform from a destitute mother worried about her daughter into a creature of mysterious beauty and sinuous movement. The firelight seemed to play off every muscle as she moved, highlighting her body as it shifted in and out of the light. Niomh occasionally made a mysterious hand gesture or gave the audience a pointed look. Each of these seemed to draw something out of that person as her dance continued, pulling them along with her. Many of the Am'ayim had found drums, pans, or boxes and were now thumping along with the music played by Baako and Jimani. The rhythm was perfect and seemed to beat with the hearts of everyone watching. Rosalie remembered reading about the Danae dance before, in Jonaas' book by Tavid the Traveler, but she had thought that the Innatraeans losing their fortunes to witness it was pure imagination. Now, she was not so sure.

While looking around the camp, Rosalie spotted Aife, who had been innocently dancing with Akua at one of the other campfires. She had stopped and was staring at her mother wide-eyed. It seemed that, given their hardships, Niomh hadn't told her daughter about her previous life as a dancer. She was sure Aife would follow in her mother's footsteps. The look on her face was pure fascination, which made Rosalie smile with joy. Their lives had changed forever, and it was a wonder to see.

Was it always like this? She remembered many tales of those her mother, Crilla, and her sister Gertrude had helped over the years and wondered if that feeling was a part of being a Weaver, too. Her mother had taught Rosalie about the hard work and dedication it took, but seeing the joy, too, brought her more hope for what her future held.

The Am'ayim felt it, too. Whatever that certain type of joy was, she could see it in their faces. These people worked hard, she had seen it on her voyage, and they celebrated the same way it seemed. Perhaps it was time to give a little something in return for keeping her safe and working so hard to get her where she needed to go. Rosalie started Weaving. The same small glow orbs she used to play games with Aife started appearing throughout the camp. Everywhere she looked, sailors were pausing in exclamation to point at them. It was marvelous to see her power being such a simple joy to those around her. She specifically noted Maleko passing his hand through a golden glow orb and laughing heartily, he was probably remembering when she'd stopped him with one during the storm.

Then Absai stopped in front of her, looking nervous, and she smiled. He was uncouth in some ways, but like all the Am'ayim sailors she'd met, he had a good heart behind all that gruff, salty exterior. "What is it, Absai?"

He smiled and reached his hand out. "Yuh woulda like fi com muv yuh badi wid mi?"

Rosalie smiled as she took his hand, letting him pull her up to join in the fun. It had been forever since she had been asked to dance or even had the chance to just let go and enjoy an evening. "I would love to dance, Absai. Thank you."

He smiled as they began to move together, and though he touched her, it was clear he was trying to be very respectful. The Am'ayim were always such surprising people. Not that she expected any difference, given her experiences with them thus far, but if there was any moment things might change, a firelit evening of drink, dancing, and music was it. "Yuh a get gud wid wi lang tawkin."

She smiled warmly, meeting Absai's eyes as they drifted apart a few places, following the tempo of the music. "Thank you. I am learning a great deal about your people. It has been wonderful."

More sailors got up and started dancing around the camp as well. The music, warmth of the campfires, and colorful light of her glow orbs seemed to combine into something more, almost like a living thing they could all feel. Rosalie remembered what Niomh had called this very physical feeling of joy, O Drom e Phirutnesko, or "The Way of Movement." Yet another new thing she had learned since leaving home was the truth of why so many journeyed to visit the Danae for festivals and how surprisingly respectful a people often looked down upon could be. Rosalie laughed as she spun around in Absai's arms, forgetting the grief she'd left behind for at least one evening.

CHAPTER NINETEEN: A WEAVER'S WORK

"**S**weetling? Come sit back down by me. It's not safe to lean over the front of the boat."

Aife looked back at her mama while resisting the urge to roll her eyes, but she went to sit back down. "Auntie Rosalie wouldn't let me get hurt, and I want to see what's happening! We were stuck on that beach for days while they fixed the ship. It was so boring."

Her mama ruffled her hair before replying, which Aife didn't like, but she was quiet about it. You had to choose your arguments sometimes. "I know, sweetling, but Rosalie is busy clearing the river so the Ariela can sail through and take us to Tursim.

Aife thought about that for a moment before replying. "I guess that's true. I remember how tired Auntie Rosalie was after saving the ship.

I wish I could have helped her!" She watched Rosalie move her arms again as another broken tree limb in their way lifted into the air, seemingly by itself and flew to the shore. "Do you think I can be a Weaver too? They're so strong, and Auntie Rosalie's ring is so beautiful!"

Rosalie looked back at the two of them for a moment and smiled. "Weavers are indeed very strong little one, but their lives are also really difficult. It is not as easy as it looks."

"I know, but I still wish I could be one too! Then I could help people like you do." Aife looked away to hide the memory of living on the streets with her mama.

Rosalie was already looking ahead again, but she replied. "The ability to Weave is something an Innatraean is born with." She looked back again, long enough for a brief smile. "Though you are still very young. Who knows what destiny has planned?"

Aife heard her mama take a sharp breath, something she always did when thinking about hard things, so she leaned against her shoulder instead of getting back up. "How do you know? Do all Weavers have rings?"

Rosalie looked back again. "Usually, the ability manifests when a child is a few years older than you. They can either do some small trick with Weaving themselves or see colorful threads of another's Weaves." She smiled. "All Weavers have rings, and as you have seen, they change throughout their lives. It is a representation of who a Weaver is."

Aife immediately remembered the night, when playing with glow orbs, that she had thought she'd seen threads. Did that mean she would be a Weaver, too? She was going to say something . . . she hadn't thought those threads were important before, but then a loud creaking came from the front of their small boat, and Rangi spoke loudly from her spot there. "Rosalie!"

Rangi was pushing a dead tree trunk with branches away from their small boat, obviously straining. Rosalie gasped and moved her hands towards it, a look of concentration coming over her face, and she turned back towards the front. "I have got it. Sorry, Rangi. Thank you." The large log, branches and all, floated into the air as Rangi let go of it and then it drifted to a nearby beach, where it landed with a thud.

Aife watched them both, fascinated. Rangi wasn't strong in the same way Rosalie was, but she was powerful too and never gave in to anything, no matter how difficult. She looked at Bayani, rowing their small boat, and smiled, remembering the day those two had fought. His only job here was to move their boat while the women did all of the work, and yet he seemed happy and calm. Am'ayim men were so different from the Aedonians she was used to. She looked back up front at the two women again. Rangi was calmly watching the river, noting every movement with her eyes, as Rosalie lifted the larger pieces of debris out of their way with her Weaving.

Even if she didn't end up being able to Weave like Rosalie, Aife could still learn to be strong like Rangi was. She was never going back to being weak and dependent upon cruel men ever again. Aife looked at her mama and smiled, she was so beautiful and strong, but in a different way than the other two women. Her mama couldn't fight or Weave, but she had survived a hard life and still protected her daughter. For now, she'd listen and let the other women do their work. "Mama? Do we have any food with us? I'm hungry."

***

Several days later, Rosalie stopped at the railing, her hand automatically resting upon the small star carved there. She'd gotten used to touching it whenever she was above deck. It made her feel like Jonaas was watching over her in some small way, which was ridiculous, of course, but feelings rarely followed logic. Then her breath caught as the Ariela sailed out into the bay, which Bez had told her was named Khalij Alshams, or "The Bay of Suns." She had thought she knew what to expect; she was wrong. The river town of Haversfjord had been interesting. It was a lot bigger than Aliselle Falls, but not like this. Her mind drifted back to all those times reading Tavid the Traveler with Jonaas back home in their barn, just the two of them imagining what the wide world of Innatraea was like. None of that had prepared her adequately for the majesty that was Tursim. The city was huge. Dozens or maybe even hundreds of small towns would fit in the mass of buildings, domes, and spires that seemed to spread across the entire bay making the landscape its own. It was as if some giant sculptor had taken the land itself, all its complex tones and hues then made a city out of it. The natural coloring ranged from tans to whites and browns, becoming brighter on the upper reaches of the taller buildings. There was color everywhere, lines of bright blues, golds, reds, greens, and even pink or black stretched across the buildings or made up the tops of spires and domes.

Everywhere the city met the bay huge quays reached out into the water, all of which were full of ships, in every size and shape she could imagine. At the end of each was a stone tower displaying either yellow or red flags that flapped in the wind, which was curious. As if understanding her question before she even asked, Bez paused next to her for a few moments. "Di flag dem signal if deh have room fi more ships an how far along di work deh. Wi a go afi wiet til maanin fi dok, kaaz no griin flag naa flai."

She nodded. How interesting! It made perfect sense as a way to communicate with ships arriving. "Thank you, Bez. I appreciate the explanation."

He nodded while tapping his pipe on the railing. "Wi can tek yuh ashore by dinghy afta we drop anchor if yuh nuh waan wait."

He and the sailors were always so helpful. The Am'ayim were very interesting people. "That is all right, Bez. I have gotten comfortable with the Ariela and her crew, and I am still tired from all of our ordeals. I will wait until we can dock in the morning." In truth, she felt at home on their ship, but it was an awkward thing to say aloud. He merely nodded while walking away and tucking his pipe into the sash at his waist. Bez was not a man of many words unless they were necessary.

She was excited to see everything and learn about the people here, despite how tired she was. From what she had read, Tursim was a rich trade city of strong laws, guilds, art, philosophy, and progress. Had she not been a Weaver and headed towards Sceotan, this would have been a good home for a woman like her. Niomh came to stand by her, with Aife in tow, to share the view. "It's a beautiful city. I think you will greatly enjoy learning about her many secrets."

Rosalie smiled tiredly. "I think you are correct. I am looking forward to all of it." She hoped that Jonaas and Edmond were both having more success on their travels than she was. Hopefully, one day, they would all see one another again. She could not hope but remember what Crilla had once said: *Weavers are powerful. This brings great responsibility because people will respect you, and with respect comes the weight of expectation. I suspect you will experience this earlier in life than most . . ."* She sighed and placed her hands on the ship's railing to prevent herself from clasping them anxiously. She felt tears but also a touch of happiness because she was heading towards her new life as much as leaving her friends behind.

Niomh quietly put her hand on Rosalie's shoulder in a show of silent support. They had learned to understand one another and became friends over the weeks aboard the ship. Aife jumped up and down next to them. "The city is so huge! How many people live there, Mama?"

Epilogue: The Politics of Hatred

"Alsiyama'nın temel kusuru, barışa ve merhamete verdiği gücün aynısını nefrete ve şiddete de vermesidir.
The fundamental flaw of Alsiyama is that it lends the same power to hatred and violence that it does to peace and mercy."
Yusef: Faith, Rebirth, and Fire

Decades ago . . .

Deniz waited patiently for the sailors to tie the ship against the dock and lower the ramp for him. They were unbearably slow, but making a fuss over it would just make the excruciating process take even longer. That's what happens whenever you challenge lesser beings with their inadequacies. He sighed; they couldn't help it. They were, after all, normal Innatraeans, inferior and pathetic. He looked around the ship at the other passengers, almost rolling his eyes. They were all so pitiful, but at least these ones had learned their proper station during the long voyage and knew their place in his presence now. He looked back out across Tursim. It was good to be home again, even if the voyage had been tiresome and his dismissal from the Greater Consensus was a ,blatant violation.

Though by the looks of things, it was good that he had come back to Tursim because it was immediately obvious that the Konsey, the council of Qin or "priests" who ruled Turism's temples, had lost influence while he was gone. There were multiple Tursi women in sight of the ship amongst the crowds, not wearing their maysaks. It was a blatant sin, a vulgar show of emotion, power, and disrespect. Because women expressing themselves in public like that meant there was a complete lack of control. There was work to do here and that meant power could be taken. This was the duty of all good men who followed Alsiyama, for with control came peace.

The other passengers allowed him to disembark first, which was to be expected—even lesser beings learned eventually. It was unfortunate that he'd had to make examples out of so many throughout the voyage. He didn't enjoy that, but it often took suffering to teach those who lacked intellect and self-control. That was his responsibility in life as a good man. Hopefully, their lessons would hold after his presence was gone from their lives. Too many fell back into Khati'ah, or intentional sin, without the presence of goodness and constant lessons.

The crowded streets were a different matter. The largest marketplace in Tursim was between him and the central temple. In places like these, a certain amount of hectic emotional behavior was expected. Even so, he felt nearly constant small spikes of irritation. He suppressed each one, intentionally pushing those emotions into Cevreleme, his Weaver's ring that rested upon the ring finger of his right hand. Each mental push added a small pinprick of light to the cosmos visible within the ring's black opal gemstone. Its name meant "containment," and this was his method of controlling emotions so that the things around him remained peaceful.

But then someone ran into him bodily, and Deniz failed to suppress his anger as he noticed new stains on his beautiful robes. He looked down at them as the offender fell in front of him. He was not one to move for or help those who were clearly inferior. Then he felt his anger rising even more because it was a woman, and worse, she was not wearing her maysak. Did the women of Tursim lose all sense of respect while he had been gone? Or did she just not see his Weaver's ring and the amulet of Qin around his neck?

But she was just noticing those very things because her eyes widened as she started to scramble away from him. The woman was in such a hurry that she left her now spilled basket of vegetables and fruits where they had fallen as she turned away and stood up to run. He tsked gently while grabbing ahold of her with weaves of air and pulling her back towards him. She landed heavily on her stomach and cried out, which was regrettable. He didn't enjoy giving out pain, but it was his duty. She started flailing with a surprising amount of vigor, so once she was even with him again, Deniz knelt by her slowly while tying her securely with more weaves of air. Having her still would make it easier to have a conversation and make it less likely that she could escape, forcing her to be more attentive. He touched her softly with the hand where his ring was and spoke gently. "Now child, you should know that trying to run away is pointless. All Innatraeans must eventually face the consequences of their Khati'ah and learn. Today is simply your day."

Deniz felt her quiver in fear against the weaves of air he had her bound with. She probably thought this was torture, but soon, she would realize that it was merely a lesson in respect. Torturing inferior beings was a complete waste of his time, but teaching them could open up new opportunities when done correctly. "Let me go! Please? I just want to go home! It was an accident!"

Deniz made his touch a little more firm and sighed again. Many tried to avoid their lessons, using fear and a desire to go where they found comfort as an excuse when what they really wanted was to go back to their easy lives. Living in Khati'ah was much easier than facing the consequences of your actions. "Why do you not wear your maysak child? You should know that showing your face in public, as a woman, is a much more serious sin than accidentally running into me." He brushed the front of his now-stained robes, feeling rather exasperated. "I might have even forgiven your staining my robes if not for your indecency."

She finally stopped trying to flail her way out of his weaves, maybe realizing it was futile. Surprisingly, the heat of anger entered her voice. "You Qin no longer rule us. We are free women! You have no right to hold me!"

Deniz sighed heavily again. She was completely delusional. Maybe Tursim had changed more than he thought possible while he was gone. He stood up and looked around the small square he'd been walking through while still holding her with weaves of air. The area was crowded now, and most of the onlookers were watching him; that was good as he was going to have to make an example out of her. He noticed many other women, a few Qin, and other Tursi, both men and women, wearing proper attire. They were watching, but no one moved to interfere; he was a Qin and a Weaver, and they knew better. Deniz nodded solemnly and closed his eyes briefly before beginning. Moments like these often defined a man's destiny and gave him the choice of who he was to become. She screamed as his weaves ripped at her dress, revealing her back, then screamed louder as the first lashes of flame landed upon her flesh. It was regrettable, but it was his duty as a moral and good man.

***

The sky was starting to darken, and Aashna needed to get home or anywhere safe, but walking was so hard. She stumbled again in pain and put her hands on the alleyway wall to hold herself up. They threatened to slip as she felt the wall become slick with her blood. She leaned against it and closed her eyes, crying. It hurt worse than anything she had ever felt before. Her entire body was covered in fiery burns and bleeding cuts, but none of that compared to what had happened. That man had violated everything Tursi women were trying to become by torturing her in public for what he perceived as sin, but the worst part was that not one person had come to help her.

Aashna tried to walk again. She had to get away from here, to go anywhere else, but her legs betrayed her, and she fell. Sinking into complete shock and utter despair, she laid her face against the rough stone wall and closed her eyes, weeping. Then she felt gentle hands embrace her and heard a woman's voice. "You're safe now. Let it out and then I will help you walk." She didn't even look up or acknowledge the words. She just collapsed into whatever woman's arms she was in and cried. The woman didn't speak again. She held her close and stroked her hair like a child while she wept, but Aashna was grateful.

Some time later, after the tears finally stopped, Aashna felt up to speaking. "Thank you. Who are you?" Her voice still felt very weak and shaky, just like the rest of her.

The woman stroked her hair again. "My name is Berezira. Hush now. You need to save your strength. You are safe, I give you my word. We will help you walk." Then she looked away at someone else. "Maryam? You and Ramineh, get your young bodies over here and help the woman up. I'm too old for this."

A much younger-sounding voice responded as Aashna felt Berezira move away from her, making room for the two younger women to help her up. "Yes, mother."

"What did I tell you about calling me that?"

"Sorry, mother."

As they helped Aashna stand, a jolt of pain shot through her body, and she gasped. "Gently, you two, she may not be as old as me, but she has at least a decade on you and is severely hurt." As they started moving more slowly, she saw another form out of the corner of her eyes come and help Berezira up, too. "Thank you Tabaan. We're both getting too old for this, aren't we?"

The other woman laughed ruefully. "Yes, we are, old friend. Let's go. We need to be inside before it gets dark."

What seemed like an excruciatingly long and painful time later, the group of women came to a large building at the end of a quiet street. Was that the south wing of the Grand Library? It had been closed for repairs a few years ago. Why were they here? Aashna was too tired to ask them though, she just hoped it was safe and warm. Truthfully, whatever awaited her here was probably better than going home, now that she couldn't perform her duties. As they neared the large door, the two young women helping her slowed even more, allowing Berezira and Tabaan to pass them. Berezira proceeded to do a strange series of knocks on the door before waiting patiently.

It was only a few moments before the sounds of a drawbar being removed came from within and then the large door opened, revealing two more women. They both nodded and moved to the side as the two helping Aashna started walking through the door. There was another pause in a room full of books as the two older women came in, and the door was closed and barred again. One of the two new women went to another door and did a similar sounding series of knocks, similar to the first door. A few moments later, it opened, and they all walked through.

This new room was massive and not full of books, but women. They were everywhere, from small children to old grandmothers, all eating, talking, reading, writing, and sewing. Aashna's mind felt too tired and foggy to comprehend what was happening. Luckily, Berezira stepped forward and took charge. It was obvious within moments why the younger two women called her mother. "Someone find me Farisa, this woman needs her skills." She pointed at someone. "You there, move, she needs that bed. Someone go get hot water and towels." She clapped her hands loudly. "Move!"

Finally, Aashna was laid down on a soft bed. She couldn't stop the tears from coming again. The pain, heartbreak, and gratitude to these women she didn't even know were too much. Another woman sat down beside her. "I am Farisa. You will be all right now. You're safe here, I promise. We will take care of you."

GLOSSARY

Aashna (Ash-nah): A Tursi woman.

Absai (Ab-eh-sigh): Bosun aboard Fi Ariela.

Aedonia (Ah-doh-nee-uh): A kingdom in eastern Innatraea bordering the Mu'ul Mountains known to conquer and absorb smaller nations, charge heavy taxes, enact strict laws, and is also home to the Holy Church of Jhoras.

Ahearne Family (Ah-hear-neh): The ruling family of Cathyor before the kingdom's fall. History says that they were all slain with their kingdom.

Ahohako (Ah-o-ai-ko): Medical purser aboard Di Ariela.

Aife (Ai-fe): Niomh's daughter, who is unusual because she has two different colored eyes, one blue and one green.

Aisna "Divine" (Ai-s-nah): A special class of Seylan citizens, often called "Companions" by foreigners. They are each specially chosen at a young age for their beauty, intelligence, empathy, and grace.

Akua (Ey-kwee-yah): Cabin boy aboard Di Ariela.

Aliselle Falls (Al-eh-see-ill): A farm town near the eastern border of Aedonia. It's located in the province of Farm Hold and is named after the nearby river rapids and waterfalls.

Alsiyama (Al-see-yah-muh): Tursi religious philosophy emphasizing control and order.

Altin Bozkirlar "Golden Steppes" (All-ten boz-keer-lar): The flat grasslands surrounding Tursim.

Amah (Ahm-ah): A Weaver of Tursi descent, long dead. She wrote "The Morals of the Weave," which is still referenced by many Weavers to this day.

Amari (Uh-mar-ee): A powder monkey aboard Di Ariela.

Amarok (Ahm-ah-rok): A Sacred Folk race that is said to resemble giant wolves.

Am'ayim, "People of Sea Mist" (Am-eye-eem): The people of the Ara'ayim Isles.

Amng (Ahm-uhng): One of the two peoples native to Amng'khor.

Amng'Khor (Ahm-uhng-kore): The southern kingdom of the far eastern region. Known for hot jungles, spicy foods, ancient temples, and strange animal-based religions.

Andalus (An-dahl-us): A kingdom in western Innatraea.

Andalan (An-dahl-un): The people native to Andalus.

Ara'ayim Isles, "Islands of Sea Mist" (Are-ah-eye-eem): Home of the Am'ayim. The isles are located far off the western coast. Outsiders are only allowed on the few larger islands outside the central waterway.

Aratohu "Guide" (Are-ah-toh-hoo): The place of a bride's father in Am'ayim wedding ceremonies.

Archibald Stallwood (Arch-ih-bald Stall-wood): The town reeve of Haversfjord.

Armis (R-mis): A man in Royal Seyla.

Di Ariela, "Lioness of the Sea" (Are-Ee-el-ah): An Am'ayim trade ship captained by Bez Masudo.

Asherah, "Lady of the Sea" (Ash-err-ah): The mother goddess of Innatraea, who gave birth to the Three Sisters.

Asherah Tree (Ash-err-ah): An ancient mythological species of tree that is the symbol of Asherah. They are believed to have provided the seeds which gave birth to Innatraea.

Asin, the "Salt" (Ah-sin): The Am'ayim native word for Innatraea's oceans. Asin also represents sacredness amongst their people, symbolizing their birth, life, and eventual death upon the sea. Mineral salt often represents protection in many of their ceremonies. The phrase can also refer to their various philosophies around life.

Atawhai (A-tah-fy): A sailor aboard Di Ariela.

Baako (Bay-ko): A musician aboard Di Ariela.

Babae ng Asin, "Woman of Salt" (Ba-ba-e en-jee ah-sin): A giant stone statue of an Am'ayim mother and child rising out of the ocean outside the Ara'ayim Isles.

Bahaghari Shell (Bah-hag-har-ee): The spiraled spined rainbow-colored shell of the deadly Papaka Kamatayan.

Bangin ng Tagak, "Heron's Rest" (Bong-een en-jee Tug-ack): The plateau-like balcony outside the main House Masudo stronghold on Ni'Moku. It is named after the large majestic birds that used to nest there.

Barth (Bart): A criminal on the King's Highway.

Bay of Swans: The massive bay near Royal Seyla's capital city of Kinrai.

Bayani (Bay-an-ee): A sailor aboard Di Ariela.

Berezira (B-air-zeer-ah): An older Tursi woman.

Bethseda (Beth-said-ah): The capital city of Aedonia.

Bezalel "Bez" Masudo (Bez-zuh-lel Muh-soo-doh): Captain of Di Ariela.

The Bond: A lifelong magical connection between Weaver and their personal Goddess Bound. It grants increased strength, faster healing, and slower aging. But it also instills a desire to obey their Weaver in all things.

Brianna Carlon (Bree-ahn-nuh Car-lawn): Edmond's grandmother.

Buhay ng Barko "A Ship's Life" (Bah-aye en-jee bar-ko): The Am'ayim belief that ship's have their own lives too.

Bundok ng Mga "Stone of Queens" (Bun-dok en-jee mah): The large ceremonial dais on Ni'Moku belonging to House Masudo. Used for important ceremonies such as the ascension of a new Reyna or marriages.

Caim, "He who drowns the weak" (K-aim): The Am'ayim god of the underneath, death, and strength. Brother of the goddess Lux.

Cathyor (Kath-yore): One of the last ancient kingdoms. Conquered by Aedonia some years ago.

Cevreleme "Containment" (Sev-rey-leem): Brother Deniz's Weaver's ring.

Chaya (Chai-uh): A woman of the Zimsway Rinowhn. Rescued by the Al'Shane family after being attacked. She died giving birth to Jonaas.

Closed Consensus: A meeting in the Great Loom of only the Greater Consensus.

Clyde (Klai-duh): A criminal on the King's Highway.

Crawley Family (Craw-lee): Family friends of the Al'Shanes. Robert, his wife Laura, and their daughter Maryanne. Robert also has a sister named Alaina.

Crilla Sharone (Krill-ah share-ohn-ay): A retired Weaver of legendary status. Gertrude Al'Shane's sister. Crilla became Rosalie Sharone's adoptive mother after finding her abandoned as a baby.

Crogwyr, "Executioner" (Cog-wee-ah): Elspeth Anwyl's sword.

Crows: Nickname for the Jhorian Crows.

Dagat ng Panahon, "Sea of Time" (Dah-gat en-jee pan-ah-hon): An Am'ayim belief that refers to an abstract Asin, or "Salt," made from the currents of destiny and fate.

Danae (Dan-ay): The semi-nomadic people who inhabit the outskirts of the vast Tanglewood. They can also be found in small numbers throughout many other kingdoms.

Brother Deniz (Den-izz): A Weaver of Tursi heritage.

Daphne (daf-nee): The Dryad connected to the Great Tree known as the Shepherd King.

Devori Mountains (Dev-oh-rye): The mountains surrounding Sophene, the eastern border of what used to be Thava, the Rinowhn Tribelands, and the Great Rift.

Djelem'den, "Pedestal of the World" or "Garden Tower" (Gel-em-den): The giant tower home of the Weavers.

Dragon Wall: A mountain range making up the northern border of Farundia.

Dryad: A Sacred Folk race. These giant feminine titans share a spiritual bond with Innatraea's Great Trees and are able to traverse between Innatraea and the spirit world known as Kanraphim.

Inquisitor Durand (Dur-and): An inquisitor of the Holy Church of Jhoras.

Dygwr Tynged, "Fatebringer" (Dye-wee-ah Tin-yed): The Ahearne Family Sword, known to have a horsehead-shaped pommel. Unique among Trefn Cyfiawnder swords because its magic can be used by a man of the Ahearne Family.

Edmond Carlon (Ed-mond Car-lawn): Childhood friend to Rosalie and Jonaas, Brianna's grandson.

Elspeth Anwyl {Els-peth Ann-wh-eel): A former member of Cathyor's Trefn Cyfiawnder.

Sister Evelyn Atwood (Ev-vel-lyn At-wood): A Weaver of Aedonian heritage. Priestess of Initiates and a member of the Greater Consensus.

Eyduan (Eh-doo-un): A sailor aboard Di Ariela.

Fadel (Far-duhl): A sailor aboard Di Ariela.

Fahz (Fah-zz): A phrase in Shatranj indicating a threat on your opponent's shah.

Fahz Nihaya (Fah-zz Nee-high-uh): A phrase in Shatranj indicating your opponent's shah is threatened and has no escape. Game end.

Farisa (Far-ee-suh): A Tursi woman.

Farm Hold: A province in Eastern Aedonia known for farm towns.

Farundia (Far-un-dee-ah): The kingdom that makes up the southwest isthmus of the continent. A land known for its juxtaposition between the rich and powerful cities around various Oasis and the mountain borders versus the savage nomadic tribes that wander its vast deserts.

Farun Da'al (Far-un-dahl): The capital city of Farundia.

Farundian (Far-un-dee-ann): The people of Farundia.

Fatiou (Fat-ee-ow): Quartermaster aboard Di Ariela.

Feorrker: A river fortress town marking the western border of Aedonia; under control of the Holy Church of Jhoras.

Fetu (Feh-too): A powder monkey aboard Di Ariela.

Fletcher (Fletch-ur): The town doctor of Haversfjord.

Flower of Ni'Moku: An Am'ayim honorific given to the heiress of House Masudo.

River of Flowers: A river in northern Royal Seyla.

Brother Frederick Alwin (Fred-ur-ick All-win): A Weaver of Aedonian heritage. A member of the Greater Consensus.

Gertrude Al'Shane (Gur-true-de Al-sheyn): Jonaas' adoptive mother, wife to Jonathan, and sister to Crilla Sharone.

Glow Orb: An orb made of bent light created by Weavers. They can vary in size and color drastically. They can also be moved about at the creator's will.

Goddess Bound: The elite irregular military organization that acts as personal bodyguards for individual Weavers. Known for the Bond, a lifelong magical connection granting increased strength, faster healing, and slower aging, it also instills a desire to obey the Weaver in all things.

Gray: The gray and black ship's vag aboard Di Ariela.

The Great Loom: The vast chamber in the upper floors of Djelem'den. It is used for meetings of the Greater and Lesser Consensus.

The Greater Consensus: The ruling body of the Weavers. This council is always composed of thirteen full Weavers, though it's rare that all of them are publicly known.

The Great Rift: A massive rift in the Devori Mountains. It borders Sophene, The Rinowhn Tribelands, and what used to be the border of Thava.

Great Tree: The commonly used moniker referring to any of the ancient giant trees around Innatraea. Most have specific names and tower over their surroundings, whether near cities or even mountains.

Guafi (Goo-ah-fee): A sailor aboard Di Ariela.

Haitasi, "The Stones" (Hai-tai-see): The My'yh's realm. Legend says that the stones here allow travel through time and location.

Hakob (How-cub): A Sophenen man who died centuries ago of old age. Crilla Sharone's first love.

Haversfjord (Hav-urs-fyord): A large Aedonian rivertrade town on the King's Highway.

Haze Flower: A psychoactive plant. It can be identified by its colorful, large flower buds and multipoint leaves. It is a very popular trade commodity, in many forms, across Innatraea.

Hiraya Masudo (H-ear-eye-uh Muh-soo-doh): Current reyna of House Masudo. Sister of Tiare.

The Holy Church of Jhoras (Jo-ras): The official church of Aedonia. It's known for its strong military, harsh judgments, political power, wealth, and hatred of those who challenge it. The Holy Church has a long history of oppressing women's power and violent conflicts with The Weavers.

Huareo (Hu-ar-ay-oh): A sailor aboard Di Ariela.

Ilo Thaj Jag, "Heart and Fire" (E-lo taj hag): Danae dance of heart and fire. An intimate dance performed for select small audiences.

Imperial Shinoda (Shin-oh-duh): The northern kingdom of the far eastern region. Little is known of this kingdom as it is isolated from the rest of the continent by the treacherous Mu'ul mountain range.

Innatraea (Ee-nah-tray-uh): The known world.

Innatraean (Ee-nah-tray-uhn): The human folk of the known world.

Iraia (Ee-rye-uh): A powder monkey aboard Di Ariela.

Isagani (Ee-sah-gon-ee): Deceased husband of Hiraya Masudo.

Jhoras (Jo-ras): The one God of the Holy Church of Jhoras.

Jhorian Crows (Jo-ree-an): The left arm, inquisitors and exorcists of the Holy Church of Jhoras.

Jhorian Phalanx (Jo-ree-an): The mighty right arm, or military, knights of the Holy Church of Jhoras.

Jimani (Him-ahn-ee): A musician aboard Di Ariela.

Jonaas Al'Shane (Jo-nus Al-Sheyn): Childhood friend of Edmond and Rosalie.

Jonathan Al'Shane (Jaa-nuh-thn Al-Sheyn): Jonaas' adopted father, Gertrude's husband.

Kai (K-ai): A powder monkey aboard Di Ariela.

Kali "Linger" (Kahl-ee): An Am'ayim fighting style that utilizes sticks called Sinawali sticks in combat.

Kaluluwa "Soul Shell" (Kah-loo-loo-wah): A shell given to an Am'ayim as a marriage proposal. They are supposed to represent who an Innatraean is and what they want.

Kamay "Creation" (Kam-aye): A cape off the coast of Ni'Mautuba.

Kanraphim (Kan-ruh-fim): The spirit world and/or afterlife. The actual beliefs vary drastically between different kingdoms and peoples.

Karum: An independent free trade town bordering the Rinowhn Tribelands and the Victory River.

Kasarena (K-ah-suh-ree-nuh): Am'ayim word for wedding.

Ka'u Malihini Taumatau "Guest Right" (Kow mal-ee-hen-ee-nee t-ow-mah-t-ow): A mostly not spoken of guest right that can be granted to foreign passengers on Am'ayim ships by request. The receiver has an assurance of fairness and protection.

Keahi (K-ee-ah-hi): A powder monkey aboard Di Ariela.

Khalij Alshams "Bay of Suns" (Khal-lij Al-shahms): The large bay Tursim is located in.

Khati'ah, "Sin" (Kot-ee-ah): Tursi word for a sinful life.

Khor River (Kore): A river in Amng'khor.

Khoran (Kore-ann): One of the two peoples native to Amng'khor.

Kievan (Key-vahn): A kingdom and people by the same name in western Innatraea.

Kidner (Kid-nehr): A man who works for Reeve Stallwood in Haversfjord.

The King's Highway: The large, well-maintained, well-guarded trade road running through Aedonia. From the northern Jhorian coastal trade city Porto de la Luce, through the kingdom's capital city of Bethseda, and all the way south to the border of Royal Seyla.

Kinrai (Kin-rye): The capital city of Royal Seyla.

Kievan (Key-von): A kingdom in western Innatraea that borders Sophene. Its people go by the same name as their kingdom.

River of Kings: A large river that flows through Aedonia from its northern coast near Porto de la Luce.

Kokoru Ista "Bay of Fish" (ko-ko-roo e-stah): The main bay of Ni'Moku.

Konsey (Kon-say): The council of Qin, or "priests," governing Tursim's religious and social matters under Alsiyama.

Korowai Feathered Cloak "Prestige" (Ko-roh-whai): A colorful feathered cloak worn by Am'ayim for important ceremonies.

Legacy: A new Weaver initiate who is sponsored by a current or retired Weaver. Many times, they are the sponsor's child.

Lesser Consensus: The collective body of all Weavers on Sceotan at any given time. They often have input on important matters, but it is the Greater Consensus that makes all final decisions.

Luau River (Loo-ah-oo): A river in Amng'khor.

Lux, "She who lights the way" (Luks): Am'ayim, goddess of the sky, light, and hope. Sister of the god Caim.

Magnus Kehlmar (Mag-nus kell-mar): A knight lord of Aedonia. He is known as a master player of the strategy game Shatranj.

Maleko (Ma-lee-ko): A sailor aboard Di Ariela.

Manaia (Man-eye-a): Helmsman aboard Di Ariela.

Manawa, "Breathe" (Man-ah-wa): An Am'ayim phrase that means it is time to rest.

Marged Llewellyn (Mar-ged Luh-wel-in): One of the few survivors of Trefn Cyfiawnder. She lives in Aliselle Falls with her two husbands, Brandon and Rory. She helped train Edmond Carlon.

River Marnah (Mar-nuh): A river in The Rinowhn Tribelands.

Maryam (M-err-ee-uhm): A younger Tursi woman.

Mataalii (Matt-all-ee): An older Am'ayim man living in Kinrai who teaches Kali.

Maysak, "Mask" (May-sak): A face covering mandated for Tursi women in public under Alsiyama.

Masina (Ma-see-nah): Pirihi, or "priest" of Caim, aboard Di Ariela.

Mundukua, "World Pool" (Moon-doo-koo-ah): Ancient magical artifacts that appear as pools of water. They allow visions of different locations and forms across Innatraea.

Mu'ul Mountains (Mewl): A treacherous mountain range that divides central Innatraea from the east, bordering Aedonia. There are a few nomadic tribes that live in these harsh climates, mainly looked at as raiders and slave traders.

The My'yh (Mai-yah): A Sacred Folk race and singular individual of incredible power. The guardian of Haitasi.

Neftali (Nef-tall-ee): Ship's gunner aboard Di Ariela.

Nehri Zengin "River of Wealth" (Nay-ree Zen-gen): "Am'ayim name for the southern region of the Victory River.

Ngakau'to Asin, "Heart of Salt" (Nah-kow Ah-sin): An Am'ayim honorific given to those of true heroism and whose heart and soul are Am'ayim.

Ni'Moku, "Isle of Birds," (N-aye-M-oh-koo): The large home island of House Masudo in the Ara'ayim Isles.

Ni'Mautuba, "Isle of Fruits," (N-aye M-au-tu-bah): An island near Ni'Moku in the Ara'ayim Isles.

Nikau (N-ee-k–oh): Galley cook aboard Di Ariela.

Niomh (Nee-ohm): A Danae woman living on the streets of Haversfjord with her daughter Aife.

Nordria (Nor-dree-uh): A distant northern kingdom of harsh mountains and ice. Made of different regions ruled by many different clans.

Nordrian (Nor-dree-uhn): The native people of Nordria.

Nordrian Ice Rose (Nor-dree-uhn): The rarest flower on Innatraea, a blue and purple rose, that only blooms during the harshest northern winters.

O Drom e Phirutnesko, "The Way of Movement" (Oh-drohm-ee-fir-uht-nes-k): Danae phrase referring to their collective knowledge of movements and dance.

Pabaybayin, "Shorebound" (Pah-baj-baj-in): An Am'ayim phrase referring to when a ship or sailor is stuck on land.

Paipa (Pie-puh): Am'ayim word for a smoking pipe.

Palani (Puh-lah-n-ee): Watch leader aboard Di Ariela.

Papaka Kamatayan, "Death Crab" (Pah-pah-kah kahm-ah-tai-yan): A deadly sea crab known for its beautifully rainbow-colored shells.

Pikni (Peek-nee): Am'ayim word for child.

Pikni ng baybayin, "Shore Child" (Peek-nee en-jee baj-baj-in): A derogatory Am'ayim term referring to children not born into Asin, or "Salt," meaning the ocean. Most Am'ayim women give birth in the surf.

Pirihi (P-ear-ee-hee): Am'ayim word for priest, shaman, or spiritual advisor.

Porto de ła Luce, "Light's Port" (Por-toe-dey-lah-loos): Aedonia's large northern coastal trade city. Known as the seat of power of the Holy Church of Jhoras.

Praeus (Pray-us): An ancient Weaver of unknown descent. Though long dead, his name is still often spoken because of his book "The Linguistics of Logic and Power," which is still respected to this day.

Qin, "Priest" (Kin): A Tursi priest.

Ramineh (R-am-een-uh): A younger Tursi woman.

Rangi Masudo (Rung-ee Muh-soo-doh): Rigging monkey aboard Di Ariela. Bez and Tiare Masudo's daughter. The Flower of Ni'Moku. Heiress to House Masudo.

Red: The orange ship's cat aboard Di Ariela.

Renfal Forest (Rinn-fawl): The forest around Aliselle Falls.

Reyna, "Queen" (Rey-na): The current matriarch of House Masudo and ruler of Ni'Moku.

Rhiannon, the Great Horse Queen (Ree-an-non): One of the Three Sisters. Goddess of the moon, wealth, power, and fertility.

Rinowhn Tribes (Rin-oh-in): The native peoples of the Rinowhn Plains.

The Rinowhn Tribelands, or "Sea of Grass" (Rin-oh-in): The vast grassland plains, mountains, and valleys that make up most of central Innatraea. Outsiders are strongly discouraged from visiting for very long by the tribes.

Rosalie Sharone (Row-zuh-lee share-ohn-ay): Childhood friend of Jonnas and Edmond, adopted daughter and legacy of retired Weaver Crilla Sharone.

Rose Apple: A hard-to-grow variety of apple that tastes similar to a pear. There are many ancient rose apple orchards near Aliselle Falls.

Royal Seyla (Say-lah): A kingdom in southeastern Innatraea. Known for being one of the richest kingdoms on Innatraea, being supportive of artists and scholars, and as the home of the strategy game Shatranj.

Sacred Folk: The collective moniker for any of the ancient mythical non-Innatraean races of Innatraea. The actual number of different races and how many are still surviving is unknown. The many stories about their magical powers and origins vary greatly between regions and races.

Salesi (Sahl-s-ee): Galley helper aboard Di Ariela.

Di Saalt (Sahlt): The Am'ayim common name for Innatraea's oceans. Saalt also represents sacredness amongst their people, symbolizing their birth, life, and eventual death upon the Saalt. The phrase can also refer to their various philosophies around life.

Sceotan (skay-oh-tan): Island kingdom of the Weavers. Located off the southern coast of Innatraea.

Sceotian (Skay-ocean): The native people of Sceotan.

Selene, The Moon Dog (Sell-een): One of the Three Sisters. Goddess of transition, roads, and the night.

Seme ando balval, "Seeds in the Wind," (S-ee-m-ee ann-d-oh b-al-vol): A Danae belief that sometimes the winds of fate must pick an Innatraean up and put them where they belong, like planting seeds.

Ser (Sehr): Honorific given to an Aedonian knight and lord.

Seraphina, The Fire Snake (Sehrah-fee-nuh): One of the Three Sisters. Goddess of fire, light, passion, and rage.

Serra (Sehr-ah): Jonaas Al'Shane's donkey.

Seylan (Say-lawn): The native people of Royal Seyla.

Shepherd King: A great tree in Aedonia bordering the King's Highway.

Shatranj (Shuh-traanj): An ancient and very popular game of strategy played on a wooden board between two opponents.

Sister Sherielle Arsenault: A Weaver of Nordrian heritage. She is a member of the Greater Consensus.

Sinawali Sticks (Seen-ah-waall-ee): The sticks used for fighting in Kali.

Sione (See-oh-nay): Ship's carpenter aboard Di Ariela.

Siofra (She-fra): A sacred folk race known for swapping human babies for their own changeling infant children.

Siua River (See-oo-ah): A river in Amng'khor.

Skywalk: A fortified city in the Dragon Wall that yards Farundia's northern border.

Sister Solange Mason (Sol-aanj may-sun): A Weaver of Seylan heritage.

Sophene (So-feen): A mountainous kingdom in western Innatraea that borders Kievan.

Sophenen (So-fin-inn): The native people of Sophene.

Tabaan (T-ab-ahn): An older Tursi woman.

Sister Taia Mirzoyan (Tie-uh mirz-oh-yan): A Weaver of Sophenen heritage. A member of The Greater Consensus and an old friend of Crilla Sharone.

Talberston's Crossing (Tahl-burr-stuns): A river town in Aedonia.

Tane (Tah-nay): A sailor aboard Di Ariela.

The Tanglewood: A vast southern coastal forest on the border of Royal Seyla, Aedonia, and the Rinowhn Tribelands. Rumors about it abound—from strange creatures, hidden cities, and magic. Many of the Danae people live on its outskirts.

Tavid the Traveler (Tav-eed): A book written by a man of the same name. The book details his many travels throughout Innatraea as well as cultural and historical information on nearly every kingdom and people, including the Sacred Folk.

Teokahl (Tay-oh-kahl): Capital city of Amng'Khor.

Thane Family (Thayn): Family friends of the Al'Shanes. Jacob, his wife Alice, and their daughter Rebecca.

Thava (thaw-vah): A once great alliance of kingdoms that took up most of northwestern Innatraea. It has now been split up into its original smaller kingdoms, one of which is Sophene.

Three Sisters (The daughters of Asherah): Rhiannon, Selene, and Seraphina. Innatraea's three sister goddesses and moons.

Tiare Masudo (Tee-ah-ray Muh-soo-doh): Wife of Bez, mother to Rangi, and sister of Hiraya Masudo.

Tubig ng Tadhana "Tides of Doom' (Tu-big en-jee tad-hanah): The Am'ayim end of the world, where gates tides eventually lead and Caim swallows Asin.

Tursim (Tur-seem): A large city-state bordering the Tanglewood and the Rinowhn Tribelands where the Victory River meets the sea. It is the largest and richest trade city in Innatraea.

Tursi (Tur-see): The native people of Tursim.

Victory River: The large river, big enough for ships to sail easily, spans Innatraea from north to south. Most of the river lies within Aedonia's borders.

Waling-waling Flowers (Wall-ing): The beautiful and delicate flowers native to the Ara'ayim Isles. There are dozens of species in varying colors, each with their meaning.

The Weavers: An ancient organization made up of those who can Weave from all over Innatraea.

Weaving: The innate ability to see the threads of magical power that make up Innatraea and manipulate them at will. It is a rare trait few are born with.

Weavers' Rings: An often threaded and gemmed ring made from unknown elements. They are also the identifying mark of a Weaver to normal Innatraeans. It is believed that each ring is unique to its wearer, the threads, symbols, or gems holding specific meanings. They have also been rumored to change over time along with their

Weaver throughout life. But in truth, little is known about these mysterious artifacts.

Whakaute, "Respect," (Wha-kow-tee): An Am'ayim gesture of respect. It involves touching the index and middle fingers to one's lips.

Yauhan ng Tadhana "Crew of Destiny" (Yah-uh-han en-jee tad-hanah): An Am'ayim phrase referring to a ship's crew that was destined to be together.

Zimsway Rinowhn (Zims-way Rin-oh-in): One of the Rinowhn tribes. They are known as Innatraea's predominant experts in Haze Flower farming.

Zuniga Stone (Zuh-nee-gah): Rough stone pendants lined with veins of blue, gold, and purple. They are somehow connected to the Zimsway Rinowhn.

Preview Novella Three:
Brenhines yn Sefyll
(A Queen Stands)

"Marw yn dda chwaer, oherwydd buoch fyw yn ddewr.

Die well, sister, for you have lived with courage."

- Trefn Cyfiawnder Farewell

About seventeen years ago . . .

Isolde stared out of the large throne room's balcony windows. Brynn was burning—her beloved city, her people's capital, and with it, the kingdom. Though a storm had begun as the afternoon came, it was too late to save them. Lightning and thunder crashed as rain fell over the flaming debris of her home that she had known since childhood. Isolde spoke in the old tongue, her people's language, even though there was no one to hear it. She needed to say farewell to them in her heart and wish them safe passage into the next world. "Marw yn dda fy mhobl, oherwydd buoch fyw yn ddewr. Farwel." Die well, my people, for you have lived with courage. Farewell. There was not much left to do. Before she died, she would see to it that her son would survive.

A queen stood; it was the Cathyoran way. She would take as many of their enemies with her as she could into the next world; there would be no mercy for their souls.

Isolde turned around when she heard them coming for her. The main throne room didn't have doors, and the invaders were loud with their lust for destruction. It had taken some argument to make her husband Cormac, their king, leave her here alone. But he also had a duty to fulfill, and she was a warrior. He knew better than to deny her this. She said a silent prayer to Rhiannon and drew Cynddaredd, or "Fury," into her hand, dropping its scabbard to the side as they entered the large throne room. The blade seethed with the crackling dark amber lightning of its hunger, wanting to devour her enemies as she raised it in challenge. "Vermin! Come and meet your end!"

To the community that helped make Innatraea possible, thank you.

Peter, Vesna, Manca, Julija, GiGi, Pouchi, Jeanine, Jean-Paul, Fil, Hétu, Irak, Marian M., George M., Todd M., Jason Bratt, Justin Bratt, C.M., Spencer P., Moriah C., Vanessa C., Brandon H. Westmoreland, Jim Chabot, Anne Chabot, Samantha Hopkins, Ron, Elaine, John, Justin, Jacob, Lori Crutchfield, Dusty Ranger, Michael B., Dawne M. Mitchell, Nathaniel L. Glenn, Lincoln Escandon, G. Reyes, Sam J., N.C., Michael Kantor, Mandy Kort.

Learn more about Innatraea!

www.innatraea.com

ABOUT THE AUTHOR

E.R. Zaugg has published several articles on being the parent of a vulnerable child, won poetry contests, and been an avid reader and world traveler for decades. His work is inspired by seeing the world and encountering different religions, spiritual beliefs, and cultures in both literature and actual journeys. These experiences have led to a body of deeply poetic work that explores what it means to be human. The Innatraea novella series highlights the value of vulnerable cultures, children, and strong women, with the goal of imparting to its readers a greater understanding and love of humanity.